DeSai

Witches Immortal

By
R.W.K. Clark

This is a work of fiction. All names, characters, locales, and incidents are
the product of the author's imagination and any resemblance to actual
people, places or events is coincidental or fictionalized.
Published in the United States by Clarkltd.
Po Box 45313 Rio Rancho, NM 87174
info@clarkltd.com

Edition 1

United States Copyright Office
TX8-281-467 May 2016
Library of Congress Control Number: 2017907101
International Standard Book Numbers
ISBN-10: 0692722165
ISBN-13: 978-0692722169
ASIN: B01GD7CVXC

/200801

CONTENTS

ACKNOWLEDGMENTS

I dedicate this novel to my wonderful readers and for all the amazing people I've met and those I haven't. To my family and loved ones, all your support will not be forgotten.

This book was made possible by reviews from readers like you.

Thank you

R.W.K. Clark

PROLOGUE

With each passing generation, this idea grew in the mind of the witches. In the beginning, it was a tiny seed, powerless in appearance, but with a great tree inside of it. As time passed, each generation played a part in its cultivation.

Vampires were as Satan's puppets; not his children, but used by him to perpetuate the death and destruction he desired to see. It fulfilled him, and he was grateful for that if for nothing else. But they were not the catalyst.

Witches, he bestowed with the power to fulfill dreams, but he gave them a major defect: they were doomed to die, and most of the time, they died terrible, horrible deaths, deaths that could not be avoided. Over time, they became obsessed with avoiding their own destiny.

This, too, was part of his plan.

It was a motivating factor that would drive them to seek a solution. The vampire was put on Earth only to give them something to seek. Rasia Engres' ancestors began to realize the chance they may have for eternal life, but it was only an idea, a theory, an out of grasp dream.

Rasia's grandmother was just obsessed enough to study. If there were vampires, what would happen if one could be found, and his eternal life harnessed? She recorded her hopes and dreams, and she passed them down.

Rasia's mother could have cared less. She was lazy and lost in dreams of love and fulfillment. She was content to work a day job and to lead her coven and raise her daughter. Her own weakness had been the death of her in the end.

But Rasia had the passion and the hatred in her heart, the greed that it would take to pursue the answers. Her grandmother had known it; she had counted on it. It had been her sole purpose to encourage her own granddaughter to carry on her work.

She had, and she was successful. Rasia would live forever, yes, and she would bear the only offspring that was spawned between a true witch and a vampire. What could the purpose of such a life be? The world was already in her possession, the world and everything in it. So now, it would belong to her child.

CHAPTER 1

Ninety years earlier

The little girl woke to the murmuring once again; she didn't startle awake, she was used to it stirring her from her sleep. She would simply rouse and open her eyes and listen to the rhythmic drone of chanting from the other room. In the end, the very sound of it would take her back to her dreams.

But tonight was different. As she lay upon her bed listening to the voices, she realized they were becoming a bit louder and more determined than usual. She had never heard them reach this pitch before, and it was enough to cause her to sit up in her bed and listen more intently.

The girl pulled her long, copper-colored hair to one side in her efforts and tilted her head toward the door of her room. All of the voices belonged to the women, as usual, but tonight they were feverish, almost desperate. They were repeating the same words, over and over, and even though she could tell they were speaking in the same strange language with which they always spoke when they held their 'meetings,' a language which she did not know, she was able to clearly make out the words.

"Purga animam suam,
Facient illam tota,
Relevare anumum,
Offernt igitur eam a mortuis!"

The girl, Anfisa, got a confused look on her face at first, but as she continued to listen to their repetition, her eyes suddenly lit up; she understood! It made no sense to her why they would say the things they were saying, but she clearly understood nonetheless!

"Cleanse her soul,
Make her whole,
Ease her head,
Bring her back from the dead…"

Anfisa threw the covers off of herself and swung her tiny three-year-old legs over the side of her bed, landing with a light 'thump' on the cold hardwood floor. She crossed the room to her door and slowly and quietly turned the glass knob until the latch workings within gave way with a small click. She cracked the door slightly, and the warm glow of light entered the doorway; the chanting voices grew even louder and more intense than before.

"Purga animam suam!
Facient illam tota!

Relevare anumum!

Offernt igitur eam a mortuis!"

Curiosity got the best of Anfisa at that point, and she opened her door just enough to creep through it, quiet as a little mouse. She tiptoed in her bare feet to the head of the staircase which led down into the common areas of the home, where she sat on the very top step and peered through the banister at what was going on at the floor below.

Anfisa saw her mother and all of her mother's friends, thirteen women in all. They stood in a circle and chanted, and as the words came from their mouths, they swayed from right to left in the light of the lanterns around them. Then the girl took notice of what was in the middle of their strange circle.

A slat of wood was settled on two of the chairs from the kitchen, and on the slat was the pale figure of one of the women's daughters, Anfisa's own cousin Lada. The sight of her older relative planted the seed of even more confusion in the child's mind, as her color was off. While one would assume she was sleeping there on that board, there was something wrong with the way she looked, and besides, who could catch a wink of sleep with all the racket the women were making who stood around her?

Suddenly, Anfisa's mother's eyes snapped open, and she looked directly at her daughter seated on the stairs. She continued to chant with the others, never missing a beat, but she held her daughter's eyes steadily. Slowly a smile spread across her face, then she closed her eyes and reset her focus.

As Anfisa looked at Lada, she noticed that the girl was beginning to get her color back. Her skin was slowly becoming more and more pink and alive-looking. She was sick, and the ladies were making her well with their words! Anfisa may have been only three, but all of this was very clear to her, and it made her feel big and strong somehow.

For the next twenty minutes, the voices continued to grow in intensity, the words never changing, but the mood and emotion reaching what seemed to Anfisa to be an almost unbearable pitch. However, the sound hurt her ears, she could not pull herself away to return to her sleeping quarters. She felt compelled to continue to watch and see what was going to happen.

All at once, Lada's eyes flew open, and she sat straight up on the board. The voices simultaneously stopped, and Lada's mother cried out loud with relief.

"Oh, my precious daughter, you are back with us now!" The woman left her spot in the circle and rushed to her daughter, embracing her passionately and weeping on her shoulder. Lada looked stunned and remained limp and silent in her mother's arms. The other women closed the gap in the circle and began to chant in Anfisa's native tongue. It sounded like they were thanking God, but the girl knew this could not be; her mother would thank God for nothing. If anything she would curse him, so who were they praising.

Finally, Anfisa got her wits about her and rose from

her place on the stairs. She ran with her tiny legs to her bedroom, and shutting the door behind her, she jumped quickly onto her bed and pulled the covers over her head. She could hear the women laughing with joy, and she knew that soon they would be leaving. She would be scolded by her mother, she was sure; all she could hope was that her mother really hadn't seen her spying from the staircase.

She lay still under the blankets listening for whatever she may hear. After a while, the house went utterly silent, and then shortly after that, she heard her mother's footsteps on the staircase. Anfisa held her breath waiting for her mother to come in and give her a tongue lashing.

The doorknob to her room squeaked as it turned, and the door creaked open.

"Anfisa. I know you are awake. It is time we had a little talk, you and I," said her mother calmly.

The girl slowly took the covers from her head and turned to her. "I'm sorry, Mama. The voices woke me."

Mother shook her head and smiled in the light of the lantern she was carrying. "No matter. You are not in trouble. Come with me down for some warm milk, child. It will help you to get back to sleep, and I can speak with you as you drink it."

"Yes, Mama," replied Anfisa, obediently. She came out of her bed for the second time that night and took her mother's open hand; it led her out of the room and down the stairs to the kitchen where her mama prepared her meals.

Anfisa did not know her papa; Mama had told her he had died at the hand of others because he had owed them and didn't pay. The home they lived in was occupied only by the two of them, and the thought of a male role model missing from her life usually never even crossed the mind of the youngster. But tonight as she sat at their meal table watching her mother pour milk into a cast iron pot over the fire, she thought about the faceless man that had been her papa. What would it have been like for him to sit with the two of them late at night, as they were doing now?

As her mama, Alyona stirred the milk in the pot, she began to sing a song to Anfisa, softly, in their native Russian language, her voice melodic and entrancing. It served to soothe the young one, even causing her eyes to droop a bit. She crossed her arms on the table as she sat on the stack of books on her chair and laid her head upon them; her mother's voice made her feel so safe and secure.

She must have dozed a bit because soon her mother was placing a crockery cup on the table before her with the warm milk inside. "Anfisa, here, drink your milk."

She sat at the table across from her daughter and began to speak softly.

"Anfisa, do you understand what you saw us doing?" The young girl held her mother's eyes, listening to her and sipping warm milk from her cup. After a moment, she slowly lowered it from her mouth and shook her head slightly.

A small smile appeared at the corners of her Mama's

mouth. "You are privileged enough to belong to a very important and powerful people, my daughter," she told her. "What you saw was one of the displays of that power. Tell me, were you afraid?"

Anfisa's eyes left her mother's as she considered the question. "No, Mama. Not afraid, just watching."

"What is it you would guess we were doing if I asked you to?" Alyona continued to smile at her daughter as she gently prodded her for the information she was holding in her mind.

Without hesitation, the child returned the smile and replied, "Making Lada all better."

Alyona threw her head back and laughed a rich, heavy laugh. When she looked back at Anfisa, her eyes seemed to be sparkling with joy. "Yes! Yes! We were making Lada all better. How do you know that, Anfisa? Who do you think told you that?"

The girl thought for a moment before looking back into her mother's eyes and saying, "I did. The me inside of me did."

Now Alyona sat back against the straight-backed wooden chair on which she sat and crossed her arms over her chest with satisfaction. "It is time for teaching to begin."

R.W.K. Clark

CHAPTER 2

Present Day

Rasia DeSai lay atop blood red satin sheets which covered a down-filled mattress. She raised her arms over her head and stretched her body from head to toe, moaning and smiling as she did. She had dreamed of her grandmother, a dream she often had, and it always made her smile upon waking. It was as though the woman was spanning space and time just to be with her and guide her.

She swung her legs over the side of the bed and sat up straight, looking around the still-darkened room. She could see clearly; the dark never bothered her anymore, not since Cyril. I should have thanked him, she thought, and the idea made her want to laugh.

Rasia looked over at the clock next to the bed. Nine in the morning. This was the very best thing about power: she could have slept for the next two days, and no one would have ever looked at her sideways for it. My, how the rules had changed. She herself had changed them.

She could remember in the beginning, when she was still searching, wandering the world seemingly aimlessly in her job as a journalist. She had never been looking for the next best story, she knew that now. She had been looking for the key, and she had found it because of her poor, deceased husband, Cyril DeSai.

The key was in her hands and her hands alone.

She stood and shuffled across the nearly pitch-black room toward her bathroom. There she turned the light on, but even that lighting was much softer than one would expect. Rasia reached her arm into the glass doors of the shower and turned on the fountain-like stream that poured down onto the ceramic tiling and trickled into the drain below. She allowed the water to flow over her hand until it reached a humanly unreasonable temperature, steam rising in great billows. She was always cold, but that went with the territory. Occupational hazard, one might say. This did make her laugh out loud.

She shed her satin sleeping gown and dropped it to the floor as she stepped into the shower and closed the door behind her. She backed her long, lithe body into the falling waters, letting it saturate her long red hair and flow down over her face. Oh, it felt magnificent as it warmed her body to its icy core.

She began to shampoo her hair, and as she did, her mind went back to her grandmother, her great-grandmother, and all the women in her line even before her great-grandmother's time. She had not known any of them, and she had known her great-grandmother only very briefly. But throughout the generations, these heroic women had strengthened the bond and the roots of who they were, who she was, and what was destined to be. They were witches, plain and simple, and they desired the great power available to rule this planet.

But alas, the evil within them brought them to terrible ends each and every time. Their bones weakened horribly, and with the passing of the years, their once beautiful faces and bodies became disfigured and horrendous to look at. Even her own striking mother, whom she had hated, had fallen victim to the inevitable end which awaited them all. Rasia would be different, though. Rasia had found the key, and she would be beautiful for all eternity.

But she knew she had to maintain, she saw the changes that were steadily taking place in her, and she knew that they were much more defined and pronounced than anything that typically happened when one was turned, as she had been by Cyril. She was far more than simply the Queen of the Vampires; Rasia DeSai was also a witch, through and through, and the combination of the different blood which was coursing through her veins made her more treacherous than any before her.

Rasia pondered these facts as she stepped from the shower. She wrapped her head in a plush black bath towel and then donned her thick red terry cloth robe. She didn't want to lose her heat any faster than she already would.

As she went back into her room, she flipped the switch and turned on the overhead light. The room was instantly illuminated with soft white light. Rasia headed to her desk in the corner and took her seat behind it. She opened a large drawer on the bottom right and took out several manila envelopes, all containing nothing but blank sheets of paper; smoke and mirrors, the envelopes were. It was what was beneath that she was interested in.

She slid a small panel from the bottom of the drawer and revealed a combination dial; the bottom was false. This was her private safe. Rasia deftly spun out the combination, and a dull 'click' could be heard from behind the door. It popped up gently, and she raised it up to reveal her Book.

It was instantly as though she felt the power emanating from its binding and pages. With both hands, she reached into the drawer, and as though with kid gloves, she grasped the Book gently and lifted it out, setting it down on the leather blotter on top of the desk before her.

It was ancient, and its appearance gave that fact away. It was bound in red leather, and a band with an intricate locking clasp kept the Book closed and kept its contents away from prying eyes. Rasia ran her hand over its cover, her eyes closed with ecstasy, her face smiling.

Now she opened her eyes and pulled out the narrow drawer that ran along the underside of the desk's main writing surface. A tiny metal key, tarnished with age, lay in one velvet-lined section of the drawer. She removed it and placed it into the keyhole on the Book's metal clasp. Rasia turned the key, and the clasp opened without a sound.

The pages of the Book were written in dark red ink. At least, that was how it would appear to someone who was none the wiser, but Rasia knew the truth. It was the blood of those sacrificed over the last several centuries. Those who had been sacrificed to appease the Earth and her ravaging hunger. The writings were clearly visible on their yellowing pages, pages which showed their age in the curling of their edges. They were parchment thin and made soft rattling sounds as she turned them one at a time.

The Book contained Rasia's lineage, and she was the last in a long line, so the Book belonged to her now. At least, it would until she could produce a daughter to carry on, but the hate in her soul kept her from pursuing that goal just yet. For now, she was simply content to gaze upon the history recorded within and revel in the truth of her existence, and she did this often.

Her great-grandmother, Alyona Alkaev. This is where she liked to begin. She had the Book and its contents memorized, but she began to relate most deeply to her own history with this woman in particular. Something about the way she ran her coven, the way she wielded her power, made Rasia almost mentally and emotionally orgasmic. Better still, great-grandmother Alyona's recording of her own life's events was spectacularly clear; Rasia would read the words and look at the drawings Alyona had put down, and she was very nearly transported to the woman's time.

Grandmother Anfisa Pajari's writings had the same

effect on her. She had been the daughter of Alyona, and she had been the one to record the theory which stated that if a witch were to discover a vampire and partake of his blessing, they could very possibly overcome the curse of their vile, ugly deaths in the future. Generations would be able to continue for all eternity, and they could practice their dark arts uninhibited. There indeed was a very good chance that they could rule the world someday.

Rasia had become obsessed with Grandmother Anfisa's studies from the second she first laid eyes on them. She had turned them over and over in her mind obsessively from that day forward. They had driven her to become a journalist because it enabled her to travel, and travel would broaden not only her horizons but her chances of finding the ever-elusive Dracula himself.

But everyone needs a safety net, and so Rasia had chosen a career she could at least enjoy. That way if she failed at her quest, she could find minute satisfaction doing what she loved. At least, next to witchcraft, that is.

Her own mother, Oksana, had been more than a burden to her, and that from a very young age. First, she tried to tell a tiny Rasia that her father had 'up and left' them, not caring for Oksana or their wee daughter enough to even grace them occasionally with his presence. She indeed taught Rasia the elementary aspects of the craft, but out of sheer hatred and disrespect for her maternal figure, Rasia had all but pushed her teachings out of her mind and far from her person. What could that wench ever teach her that she couldn't learn for herself?

So she had taken the Book from her mother upon her own death, as was commanded by their predecessors, and began to record her own experiences upon its remaining blank pages. The blood was not that of sacrificed virgins, granted, but it was the blood of the many male victims she left strewn across the vast landscape of her life, and this fact did not bother her in the slightest. So she had deviated from The Way; this meant nothing to her. She would continue on her course to prove (or disprove) Anfisa's beliefs once and for all.

Rasia turned the next page of the Book. It contained the tale of, her grandmother, Anfisa's own daughter, Oksana's life and learnings. This was Rasia's mother Oksana, and she had been the true groundbreaker of them all.

While Anfisa had spoken of Dracula and the potential behind taking in his blood, Oksana had taken the theory to an entirely new level. She killed simply for the sake of obtaining the life's blood that only her victims could provide. In this way, she began the true hunt for the one true 'Vampire' that could give this feminine lifeline an eternal existence. Oksana Engres had been determined, and she didn't care who had to die during the course of her quest.

For the entire sum of her days, Rasia had continued the journey, had continued the hunt. She would find the bloody 'fountain of youth' that her ancestors had diligently sought, and she eventually had found it in Cyril DeSai. As she cast her eyes on the pages of the ancient Book and stroked its cover with her fingers, her mind went back to her own search for eternal life and boundless power...

CHAPTER 3

Thirty years ago

Oksana Engres brushed her hair before the vanity mirror, taking each stroke slowly and deliberately. She did not smile, nor did she take her eyes from the hairbrush or her hand, but it was not the task she was busying herself with that filled her mind. She was thinking about her husband, Arkady.

Things had begun beautifully for the both of them. There had been an abundance of love and laughter. His family loved her, and though she had no family of her own, she was sure they would have loved him, as well. They had wed just seven months ago and set up house in this very apartment, and until last week, their entire relationship had been nothing short of idyllic.

She had discovered her pregnancy ten days ago, and she had told Arkady the wonderful news over a candlelight dinner. He had been ecstatic; they had both wanted to start a family as soon as possible, and the news of Oksana's pregnancy delighted the young man.

But the very next night, while Arkady slept, Oksana had begun to engage in a minor sacrificial rite which would not only ensure the health of the child she carried, but it would also guarantee the birth of a female child. To a true witch, this was terribly important; a male child being born first would throw things all askew for her line.

But Arkady had heard her chanting; it had roused him from his sleep, and he had risen to investigate the sounds. He stood under cover of darkness in the hallway and observed his beautiful young wife dancing naked in the light of some candles she had burning, and she had been singing and chanting in a strange tongue, uttering words which he did not understand in the slightest.

But the fact was not only that her behavior filled him with a sense of dread, but he also saw the bloodied body of a young girl lying on the floor in the center of a pentagram. Once he took notice of the dead child, he had shot from the darkness and grabbed his wife by the shoulders, spinning her around violently and shaking her.

"Oksana, what have you done? What are you doing?" He could think of nothing else to say, he was at such a loss for words.

She had instantly snapped back to reality, and once she grasped that he had caught her in the middle of her craft, she began to laugh uncontrollably. The look on his face became one of sheer horror.

She controlled herself and looked into his eyes in the flickering light, still smiling. "I am ensuring that our daughter is born full of power, Arkady. Don't be afraid; my family line affords me the strength and ability to do this."

His eyes scanned her face. "You are a witch, Oksana?"

Once again, the young woman laughed. She was unsure what else to do; reality was the reality. Her mother Anfisa had warned her that this day would come, and she had also warned her that chances were great that no husband would accept the truth, but even as these thoughts passed through her mind, Oksana was sure that her love, her Arkady, would be fine with the facts.

"I am, my love. I come from a very long line. There is nothing to fear; we will prosper together because of my lineage," she answered.

But now, it was Oksana's turn to be surprised. Arkady turned from her and turned on the overhead light, and when he turned back to her, his eyes were filled with rage.

"Who is this child, Oksana?" Suddenly, she knew her marriage was destined to end just like that of the women before her.

Now she narrowed her eyes, and the smile disappeared from her face. How dare he interrupt her rituals? How dare he even question her motives or behavior while angry? Her naked body began to move slowly away from him, and she circled him slowly.

He didn't seem to notice the change in his wife's demeanor. He rushed to the body lying on the floor, and he knelt down to inspect the dead child more closely. He then looked up at Oksana.

"I will call the police," he said simply.

Suddenly she saw red. To take away her sacrifice would only result in a stillbirth, and this she would not tolerate. Arkady had turned his attention back to the lifeless body on the floor, and she took the opportunity to retrieve the knife she had used on the girl from a small stand near the kitchen door.

Before her husband even knew what hit him, she attacked, first reaching around and slicing his throat in one deft movement. She then proceeded to stab him continually in the back, shoulders, and neck, her own body finally collapsing to the floor in exhaustion. When she gained her senses, she looked to where he lay; it would be best, she thought, if his body had landed in the pentagram.

It had, and this made her smile.

Oksana stood and turned out the overhead light and resumed her dance. Soon she was chanting once again, and the energies were flowing more powerfully than ever. The Powers were pleased with this double sacrifice, just as her mother Anfisa had told her they would be if it ever came down to this.

She had done correctly.

Now, just over one week later, she sat brushing her hair in the apartment, and she felt no sense of loss over Arkady. She knew that in several months, she would have a beautiful daughter. In the meantime, she would prepare for the birth. She knew, deep inside, that this child would be the one to see the fulfillment of the dream held by herself and her ancestors.

This child would find the vampire; this child would bring eternal life and power to their kind.

∞

Oksana stood from the vanity and sat upon the edge of her bed. She was more tired than usual, and she attributed this to her condition. As she made herself comfortable on the bed, her mind turned to the reality of her own loneliness. It was not a feeling she was experiencing because Arkady was gone, no, it was simply Oksana. Her own mother had told her that if she did not learn to live with the loneliness, it would cause her terrible problems.

She finally began to doze off, with dreams of a man with no face drifting through her mind. Oksana was addicted to love and lust. It would fill her dreams for the remainder of her life.

∞

For the next eight months, she worked cleaning houses, and she kept her eyes and ears open and in tune to any and every man around her. Not only was she half-heartedly searching for the ever-elusive vampire, but she was also looking for a mate that would love and accept her for who she was. She looked and looked for the entirety of her pregnancy.

She was prepared regarding what she would tell her daughter about her father: he deserted them. He did not want to care for his wife and young daughter as a man should, and he simply disappeared one day. This was the story she told everyone else, as well, and it appeased each and every person who came asking after him, including the police when she had reported him missing. After all, men shirked their responsibilities so often in this day and age. No one was truly surprised.

∞

Oksana went into labor alone, and she delivered her beautiful Rasia. She was born on a cold December day with hair the color of fire, just like Arkady had, and even though her eyes were emerald green, they blazed with flame as well. The child was perfect; Oksana couldn't have been more blessed. It was a good thing she had rid her life of Arkady for the sake of their daughter.

As for Rasia, she was bright and driven from day one. She could remember instances from a very young age, and she was quick to learn the lessons her mother taught her. For the first few years of her life, she was very, very close to Oksana; the two did everything together, and it was safe to say they were the best of friends, not just mother, and daughter.

But after Rasia turned five and began her formal schooling, things changed at home. Oksana had begun to take boyfriends. Rasia knew there was nothing inherently wrong with this, for almost all of the children at her school had both a mother and father figure in their lives. The problem was the men Oksana chose.

Initially, her relationships were simple flashes in the pan, but because they were so short-lived, the woman seemed to search all the harder. They would end for a variety of reasons, ranging from the boyfriends trying to direct Rasia around the house, to them fighting over the weekly meetings her mother would have at night with the other women. None of the men stayed around for long.

Then, when Rasia was eleven, everything changed.

It happened on a spring day. The month was May, and the flowers were blooming colorfully everywhere she looked. She loved walking home from school during these months when it was not too cold and not too hot. She had no real friends to speak of, and her walks gave her time to think and plan. She had dreams for her future. She wanted to write for a newspaper.

She had arrived home this particular day feeling very cheerful and content. Her mother was not home when she got there, which was not unusual. Oksana had to work many hours to pay the bills for herself and her daughter.

While her mother was not there, her mother's boyfriend was, however. He was the latest in a long line, and he was a bit younger than those who came before him. His name was Stephan, and he had been seeing Oksana for just under two months.

There were things about Stephan which proved to give Rasia an unsettled feeling. First, she did not like the way he spoke to her mama. He tended to demand, and he never said please. Sometimes, if Oksana did not cater to his whims quickly enough, he would sneer, and once Rasia had even heard him refer to her obscenely.

Secondly, he looked at Rasia in a way that made her stomach feel a bit sick. She had begun to develop breasts, and on more than one occasion, she caught him staring at them. This moved her to cover them or leave the room, which always seemed to make him chuckle. Rasia could not wait until this relationship fell apart like all the others.

But today, Stephan was still around, and not only that, he was at Oksana and Rasia's home without her mother. As soon as she walked into the door and realized the circumstances, her stomach sank. Something bad would happen this day, she just knew it.

She had come into the apartment and gone directly into the kitchen to look for a snack. The place was still; no television or music played, and there were no lights on. Even the curtains were closed.

Rasia rummaged through the small refrigerator and found a bit of cheese that would go well on some crackers. She was in the middle of slicing it at the counter when she heard a noise behind her, which caused her to turn suddenly.

There stood Stephan, a wide smile splayed across his lips. "Hello, Rasia," he leered. "How was your day at school?"

Rasia had looked down at the knife in her hand before looking back at her mother's boyfriend and answering. "It was fine today. It is a beautiful day outside. Have you been out?"

The man continued to smile as he made his way into the kitchen, taking a position behind the girl. "Yes, Rasia. After all, I had to get here, did I not?"

"Yes, yes. I guess I wasn't thinking, sir." She turned

her attention back to the cheese, slicing the last bit of it up for her snack.

Stephan chuckled, and Rasia felt him get closer to her. She could smell alcohol coming off of him in waves. Was he already drinking? After all, it was just now three-thirty in the afternoon. Her skin crawled a bit, and she shifted her weight from one foot to the other nervously before turning around to reach for the box of snack crackers her mama kept in the cupboard.

But Stephan was so close to her now that she succeeded only in bumping right into him. He put his hands on her shoulders and looked her in the eyes. He was so close to her she could see spittle glistening on his bottom lip, which was quivering a bit.

"You should be more careful, Rasia," he began. Suddenly his right hand went from her shoulder to her budding left breast. Her stomach lurched violently; the man was making her sick. She did not feel nervous, rather, she felt fury and hatred was over her in waves.

She drew back her right hand and tightened her grip on the knife she held in it. His mouth was suddenly on hers, and his hand continued to stroke her chest. She plunged the knife into his stomach before he even knew what was happening. His head snapped up, and he looked at the child in shock. It was Rasia's turn to smile now.

She pulled the knife out and stabbed him yet again. Now the man's hands went to hers, but he was unable to stop what had already been done; his blood was pouring from the wound in his stomach and spilling to the floor.

Rasia turned the knife as she sneered at him.

"Did my breast feel good to you, Stephan? Yes? Well, how does this feel?" Rasia asked him, her voice filled with amusement.

The man simply fell to his knees where he stood. Rasia removed the knife from his belly and tossed it into the sink with bloody hands. She watched as Stephan fell face first to the floor, a trickle of blood escaping from his mouth as he breathed his last.

Rasia stepped calmly over the man's body and washed her hands at the sink before fetching her crackers from the cupboard. It simply wouldn't do to eat with bloody hands. Her mother would have told her that. She took her snack and sat at the small table in the dining room, a smile glued to her face, and patiently waited for Oksana to return home to help her clean up the mess on the kitchen floor.

CHAPTER 4

That day had been the beginning of a brand new life and perspective for Rasia Engres.

Oksana had returned home, and while one would think Rasia would be bracing herself, she was not. Her mother walked into the apartment to see her daughter sitting calmly at the table eating her after-school snack.

"Hello, dearest," Oksana had begun. "How were your lessons today?"

Rasia chewed her mouthful and swallowed before responding. "Fine, Mama."

Her mother had gone about hanging her light jacket and putting her purse in its place next to her lounger. She then came to the table and stroked her daughter's hair as she bent down and planted a kiss firmly on her forehead. She then turned toward the kitchen; Rasia put the last bite of cheese and cracker into her mouth and began to hum to herself as she chewed.

"Rasia, what has happened here?" her mama calmly asked.

Rasia swallowed her food again. "Stephan touched me. It made my stomach ill." She resumed her humming.

"Where did he touch you, Rasia?" Now her mother was standing next to her.

"My chest," the girl replied.

Oksana nodded and took a breath. "If you are finished eating, I will need your help to clean this mess up."

With that, the two proceeded to clean up the blood from the kitchen floor. Oksana moved Stephan's body out of the way, placing it atop a couple of black garbage bags she had spread out. Once the blood had been cleaned up, they dragged his lifeless body out the back door, and after a bit of a struggle, managed to get his body across the fenced-in yard, and into the river.

"I will take care of the rest after you go to bed tonight. There is nothing more you can do, but we must talk," she told her daughter.

They made their way to the dining room, where Rasia took a seat at the table and waited for her chastisement, but chastisement was not what she received. Her mother stood just inside the kitchen and began to prepare dinner, speaking to her the entire time.

"If you are old enough to take a human life, you are old enough to know who we are. You are old enough to know our history," Oksana began. She put a lid on the pan on the stove before standing on a stepstool and fetching what appeared to be a very old Book from the top of the cupboard. She then came into the dining room and took a seat across from Rasia.

"Rasia, you are a very special girl. What has happened here today has proven your strength and power to me. Now it is time for you to know exactly who you are so you can continue the work that must be done," Oksana said.

Rasia held her mother's gaze, gooseflesh-raising all over her body. "I already know what I am; you do not have to tell me that. I have always known: I am a witch, just like you."

"How did you know that?" Oksana asked her.

The girl shook her head. "I don't know how. I just know what I know in my mind and my heart, but I don't really know what that means."

Her mother breathed a sigh of relief, but she continued to look at her daughter warily as if trying to weigh out the words she had spoken. "Very well. You have an ocean of knowledge that has been gifted to you, but it is time for me to teach you about your history, as well as your future."

For the next several hours and well past Rasia's bedtime, she and her mother talked about the long line of witches that Rasia had come from. They discussed the contents of the old Book that her mother had retrieved from the top of the cupboards. In it were the writings of those before her; they had recorded their lives, as well as their goals, the main one being to locate a vampire if indeed they did exist.

"That is your destiny, Rasia. Do you understand that?" Oksana asked.

Rasia nodded then. "Oh, yes. I understand all you are saying. To find the vampire means we will not only have power, but we will never die."

Her mother's eyes lit up with excitement. "Yes, Rasia! I have you, so my search has been very limited," she replied. "But you do not have to be hindered by the circumstances of life if you choose not to."

"What must I do?"

Now her mother told her how important it was to never trust a man and to never allow the love emotion to dictate her choices. To have a child would slow the process, even though it would be vital if their line were to be continued. She told her she must choose a career that would make the search easier. She must gain as much education as possible, and she must feed the blackness in her soul until it becomes her master.

Later that night, Rasia lay in her bed and listened to the sounds of her mother in the kitchen tending to the blood of that scum Stephan. How bright her future suddenly seemed! Rasia knew that she had a purpose, and she would fulfill it. Her ancestors may have failed, but Rasia would succeed; she would see to it.

If a vampire existed, Rasia would find it, and she would steal its power of life eternal. She would possess it, then she would rule the world.

CHAPTER 5

As a young adult

High school had passed pretty much uneventfully for Rasia Engres. She dated a few boys, but as soon as they got a little handy with her, she had stopped seeing each and every one. She couldn't continue to kill everyone who touched her; her mother had made sure she understood that. If she did, it would stop her quest before it even began.

Instead of becoming emotionally invested in anyone, she spent much of her free time studying her own history, as well as that of the ever-elusive vampire. Did they really exist, or were they simply the things horror stories were made of? She was determined to find out for sure, and so she committed herself to the gaining of knowledge her goals would require.

During her high school years, she also began to participate in her mother's coven, becoming a very active part of it. Oksana taught her all the spells she would need, but Rasia took it upon herself to learn even more. Her mama was accomplished in the craft by her own right, but Rasia was determined to surpass the woman's level by leaps and bounds.

While one would think a mother and daughter like Oksana and Rasia would be emotionally close, nothing was further from the truth. Her mother loved her deeply, she knew, and from the woman's perspective, they were very close. But the fact was that Rasia despised her mother for the weakness she had when it came to men. Her preoccupation with this type of interpersonal relationship had caused her to neglect the goals held by her ancestors for literally centuries.

Because of her determination to succeed, she focused on not only soaking up knowledge regarding witchcraft but everything else she could get her hands on as well. Her past desire to become a journalist was fitting; it would provide her with ample life opportunities to continue her family's search for a vampire.

By the time she graduated high school, she had chosen to attend college at Kyiv International University in Kiev, Ukraine, and she managed to ace all testing required for her admission. She would major in Journalism, with a minor in Foreign Politics, for she believed this would be a major help when it came to her search.

She looked at it this way: anyone who would live forever, and be a murderer by very nature, at that, would come to power somewhere, at some point. This was why she believed journalism would be the best career choice even now. If she worked hard, she would be able to pursue assignments involving only the most prestigious, and that was going to be vital to her success.

Now, twenty years old, and Rasia Engres was half-way through her formal college education. While the other students partied, got laid, and had fun, she was constantly busy with her studies, even taking a job at the paper in the mail room just so she could gain a bit of extra knowledge. She had no interest in off-time activities; Rasia would have plenty of time for that when it was all said and done.

It was during this, her sophomore year, which another major life event occurred for her, showing her what she was really made of. Rasia would experience true competition for the first time in her life, and the way she handled it really said it all for her. She could literally handle everything that came her way, regardless of the resistance it presented her with.

She studied English, Japanese, and German, mastering each before moving on to the next, and then she dabbled in other languages. French and Italian seemed to come naturally to Rasia, and her dabbling proved to benefit her even further. It was during one of her language classes that she met Mahlis Porkov, another student who was determined in her studies. Mahlis was just determined enough to step on anyone who posed an interference with her own life goals.

Mahlis was to become a physician, and she wanted to practice overseas. Where really didn't matter, so she, like Rasia, took as many foreign language courses as her already packed schedule would allow. It was during their time studying Italian together that the two girls were assigned to a study group together.

The main assignment for each group was to write a script entirely in Italian. It was to showcase both of their majors in a way that would detail their studies to an audience for whom the script was performed. Rasia felt that journalism should be the primary topic, with the medical student's role being a bit downplayed; Mahlis wanted the focus to go the other direction.

During the third week of the project, things became a bit heated between the two. Mahlis had even given into Rasia a bit; she would take the least bit of attention, as long as her role was portrayed with thoroughness. Rasia had simply smiled and agreed.

So the two set about writing the separate parts. They would then combine them into one solitary story together, finding the balance as they went. This was the agreement, at least, and Rasia had even given in willingly and with what appeared to be eagerness. Little did Mahlis know that Rasia really never gave in to the desires of those around her in any way that was overt.

Two days before their script was to be turned in, they met together and conferred on the assignment. They were short on time, and Rasia took advantage of this fact by not only agreeing to everything Mahlis said, but she also offered to carry the brunt of the work by melding both scripts together and preparing the final assignment. She would do all the word processing, leaving Mahlis to focus on studying for an anatomy test. They went their separate ways, both smiling.

But Rasia sat in her own vehicle as they left the library that day. She watched as Mahlis got into her car.

She watched as the girl turned over the ignition, and she watched as the car blew sky-high, taking the medical student with it. Rasia simply smiled as she pulled out of the parking lot, driving slowly through the crowd that was gathering among the wreckage that had been Mahlis' car.

That night she compiled the final script for their assignment, and she took advantage of the death of her study partner. Not only did she give Mahlis the majority of the attention in the script, but she managed to earn the class' top grade. She had used her partner's horrible death, writing it into the script to successfully bring out the emotions of her classmates and professor.

It had worked out so much better than she thought. Rasia Engres knew that nothing in the world would be able to stop her from achieving her goals, not even a determined, intelligent classmate. Her time had not even come yet.

Not only did her years at the University prove to educate Rasia for her future career choice, but it was also during this time that she would become more alert and attuned to the people of the world for the sake of finding a true vampire. She kept her ears and eyes constantly open to anyone who would fit the bill that her mother and grandmother had given her, but locating such an individual would not prove to be an easy task. Combined with her studies and career focus, she simply did not have the time to devote to it that she would have liked, but Rasia consistently kept her radar going, and she was very, very careful to keep this business to herself.

She visited numerous libraries and soaked up as much knowledge about vampire history and theory as she could get her hands on. She shoved fictional accounts aside; she wasn't at all interested in romantic fantasies about sexy monsters. She wanted to find the real deal if it indeed did exist. If there were a vampire walking the face of the Earth, she would find it, male or female, and she would take the steps necessary to harnessing their power and keeping it all for herself.

She did not do much traveling for the sake of her vampire studies during the furthering of her education; she just didn't have the time. The time she was able to invest, she dedicated to books and documentaries. Because of her high level of secrecy, she didn't even go so far as to track or interview so-called professionals. Any information she needed would come to her in her own time when it would be most useful and appropriate, of this she was sure.

She watched politicians and businessmen, but her concentration was mostly absorbed by her studies. For the entirety of her time at the University, no one, in particular, caught her eye, though there were a couple of individuals who she would have preferred to discover as being her vampire. Something always set her right in her small suspicions, however. During her professional training, the identity of any true vampire would remain just out of her grasp.

∞

The final two years of her studies actually stole even

more time from this extra-curricular activity. Now she had more testing and more in-depth topics to learn than ever before. Her time became more and more consumed by needing to focus on these things, as well as internships which she desired to fill for the experience. The times when she was able to delve into a bit of literature on the topic, her roommate at the dorm would tease her incessantly, referring to her as a 'lover of the horror genre.' The girl saw Rasia as being preoccupied with a pipe dream, but she knew better.

She would ignore the digs. She knew the reasons that she was driven to read up and study the topic: Rasia needed to know all she could about the facts if facts even existed. There were times she had her doubts. Perhaps her mother and grandmother were out of their female minds to even have such pie-in-the-sky ideas. Even when she became tired of searching, though, she knew in her heart that this individual must exist; the Powers had placed the dream into her grandmother's heart. It was the responsibility of this line of women to pursue it.

She continued with her college education, and she made sure that her future and career remained the top priority. After all, it would be along these lines that she believed she would eventually be permitted to discover this… ghost. But this did not stop her from always looking, always seeking, in one way or another, no matter how little time she had to invest.

The answer would come. When it did, she had full confidence in the Powers that it would fulfill her every need and desire, but for the time being, she chose responsibility over these hopes and dreams mainly. She would demand that patience work for her, not against her, and certainly not against the charge that had been handed down to her from her ancestors. No, she would continue to seek, she would simply take her time doing it. There would be a fine balance that would need to be carried out, and Rasia would see to it that this balance was maintained, for the sake of the Greater Good.

CHAPTER 6

November, Winter Break

"Why France, Rasia? The last time you spoke of taking your break off campus, you said you were interested in Germany. Why the change of heart?" Anastasia Malkov, Rasia's roommate, was sitting at the foot of her bed watching her pack her single suitcase full of clothing and toiletries.

Rasia smiled at her. "I guess, taking French sparked an interest I never knew was there. Besides, they have some wonderful wine in France, and you know how I feel about that."

She closed her case and sat on top of it to get it to close and fasten more easily. "Will you see if my cellular phone has a full charge, please?" She bounced a couple of times on the lid before she was able to close and lock the clasps.

Anastasia picked up the unit from the nightstand between their beds. "Yes, it's full. Are you sure you don't want to visit my parents with me for a holiday? You don't always have to spend your breaks alone, you know."

"I know, I know. I'm not really using this time for a

holiday. I'm doing a bit of side… journalism work. That way I'm on top of things before finals and graduation this spring." She moved her case to the door. "Mikhael wants to have a drink with me tonight in town before I leave. Do you remember him from Debate?"

Anastasia nodded disinterestedly. "Are you going?"

Rasia smiled once again. "Yes."

Now her roommate got a strange look in her eye. "Rasia Engres, I have never known you to date! Have you found love?" The girl grinned and got a dreamy look in her eyes. "If so, I would say it is about time!"

The journalism major simply shook her head. "No, love has nothing to do with it. He is going to give me some information on safe places to stay in the area I am visiting. He is also going to tell me about some good places to eat there. His family has relatives a short distance from there, and he has visited the area a number of times himself."

Now Rasia stood at the mirror over the bathroom sink. She brushed her long red hair and freshened her makeup a bit. "My plane leaves at eight-thirty in the morning. I'll be back here pretty early, so if you intend to be gone, please make sure you shut the computer off."

Anastasia nodded, and the two said their goodbyes to each other. Rasia grabbed her purse and left the dormitory room, heading to the local bar. The night was warm and breezy; she would have loved to walk, but it would take much less time to drive. She took a deep breath as she unlocked her car and gave into a necessity.

When she arrived at the small tavern, her friend was already there waiting for her. She ordered a glass of Shiraz, her favorite wine, before settling in across the table from him.

"Hello, Mik. How are things going for you?" She removed her light sweater and hung it over the back of her chair before taking her own seat. "Thank you for meeting me and telling me about France. I am anxious to go."

Mikhael winked at the beautiful girl who sat with him. He had already drunk three beers, so he was feeling more comfortable in her presence than he ever had before. Usually, just the sight of her was enough to make him forget his own name. He wound up stumbling over his own words whenever Rasia Engres was near.

A blonde waitress wearing blue jeans and a cropped shirt came to their table and set Rasia's glass of wine before her on a napkin. She paid the girl and then turned her attention to the wine and Mik. Rasia waved the glass under her nose, closing her eyes as she inhaled its aroma. A smile formed across her lips. This wonderful red would do. She lifted it to her lips and took a sip, swishing it around over her tongue before finally swallowing and speaking to her companion. "So, tell me about the place I will be visiting."

For the next hour, Mik filled her in on the French town she would be staying in. He made her aware of just about everything he could think of, even providing her with a list of homes that let out rooms and restaurants with quality food. After an hour of friendly conversation, Rasia ordered another glass of wine and excused herself to use the restroom. While she was gone, she thought about why she had chosen France for her holiday. She wasn't entirely sure. She did love her wine, and she felt excited at the prospect of visiting the country, but there was also something deep inside that drew her, or at least, that was how she felt. She would go with the feeling. Not to mention she had read about a few rumors of an ancient vampire from the area.

She returned to the table, smiling. "So, how are your studies?"

Mik blushed slightly before responding to her. "Well, I am no scholar, like yourself, but I am keeping my head above water." He was studying journalism as well, but he was a bit behind in his classes, the last she knew. "I was hoping when you returned from France, you would be willing to help me bail myself out by tutoring me in a couple of subjects."

"Surely. I would be happy to," she replied as she lifted her glass to her lips. She took a healthy swig from her fresh drink and said, "Do you have any job leads for after graduation?"

Mik was watching her calmly. "Yes. A station up north has offered me an internship. With your help, I will be more than prepared." He was keeping a close eye on her now, and his smile had all but faded.

"Are you okay, Mik? You seem to be a bit... distracted since I came back," she said.

He blinked rapidly. "No, I'm fine. You look a bit

pale, Rasia. Are you okay?"

She had just finished the last of her second drink, and stood to go as he spoke, but no sooner did the words come out of his mouth than she was overcome with vertigo. She grabbed the back of her chair and used it to guide herself back into a sitting position. She shook her head back and forth in an effort to clear it; her vision was slightly blurred, and her mouth was paper dry.

"I guess I feel a bit funny, but it will pass. Just give me a moment," she told him.

Mik continued to stare at her, and she was becoming more and more 'detached.' In her confusion, she noted vaguely that he didn't look concerned; he simply looked cautious.

"Did you drive here tonight, Mik?" She asked this because she knew she couldn't drive her car the way she was feeling. Why was she so dizzy? She should've been able to drink another two drinks easily. She thought of her flight in the morning. "I need to get back to the dorm, and I don't think I should drive."

Mik shook his head. "No. I walked. Did you drive? I can take you back in your car if you like," he told her.

She nodded and stood, still steadying herself on the chair. She grabbed her purse in one hand and her sweater in the other as Mik took her by the elbow and gently guided her toward the door of the tavern.

Once they were at the car, Rasia rummaged in her purse and fished out her car keys, which she handed to her friend. "Thank you so much, Mik," she said. "I don't know what I would do without you."

"No problem," he replied as he helped her take her seat. He reached across her to help her fasten her safety belt, and Rasia felt his hand brush against her breast. It lingered there too long.

Soon they were pulling away from the curb and heading in the direction of the dorm. Rasia was resting with her eyes closed and her head back, but when she opened them again, she saw they were actually on the outskirts of town.

She knew.

"Did you want to take a drive, Mik? You should have just said something." Her voice was slurred, and she noticed this brought a smile to his face. The fact was she had added the slur. If Mik were in search of a good time, she would make sure he got one.

"Just rest your eyes. Before you know it, you will wake up, and it will be time to go to France," he told her soothingly.

She did as he suggested, but she maintained clear consciousness. She was a bit nauseous, but with each passing moment, it seemed that her vertigo was improving. She opened her eyes slightly; they were in the country now.

The roads grew darker as night fell, and as the darkness came, the interior of the car dimmed as well. Very carefully, Rasia allowed her purse to drop to the floor while letting her arms and legs go lax. She took notice of Mik looking over at her. He thought she was passed out cold. Good, she thought to herself. Keep thinking, dirtbag.

Soon Mik turned off the road and pulled the car over and turned off the ignition. She heard the driver door open and close again, so she opened her eyes briefly. He was making his way to her side of the car. She closed her eyes just as he opened the door, and he sat on the edge of her seat next to her.

Suddenly his hands were both on her chest, and he was shoving his tongue into her mouth. She opened her eyes and slurred against his mouth, "If you wanted to have fun, why didn't you just say so?"

Upon hearing that, Mikhael was beside himself. He began to take off his shirt as fast as he could. "No, Mik. I want to taste you in my mouth," Rasia said. Even in the darkness, she could see his eyes light up as he jumped to his feet and began to unbutton his jeans as fast as he possibly could.

"I knew you liked me, Rasia. Sometimes girls like you just need a little encouragement, that's all," he said as his pants fell down around his ankles.

Rasia straightened herself with exaggerated clumsiness and leaned toward Mik. She took his small, erect penis in her hand. It was all she had in her to keep from laughing out loud, but she kept her amusement to herself. She wrapped her lips around him and slowly began to work her tongue.

Mik's knees slammed together almost immediately, and he let out a deep, guttural moan. That was Rasia's cue. Before he even knew what was happening, she bit her teeth clean through his poor excuse of manhood.

Blood filled her mouth as he screamed. He tried to drop to his knees, but her hold would not permit it. Now she looked up at him in the light of the small lamp on the roof of the car interior. His face was filled with horror, and his face was ashen.

She spat his flesh onto the gravel road and subconsciously licked his blood from her lips before wiping her mouth with the back of her hand. "I don't suppose you'll be needing a ride back to your own quarters, will you now Mik?" she asked him. She got out of her car, a little wobbly on her feet, and made her way to him.

"You know, you piece of crap, you really did me a great favor here," she said as she grabbed his arm and yanked his pain-wracked body from the car. He fell to the gravel and dirt and rolled over on his back, moaning and sobbing in his plight. Rasia didn't waste any time. She made her way to the front of the car, and by the light of the headlamps, she drew a rough pentagram in the dirt of the road. She staggered a bit in her efforts, and in her mind, she prayed that the Powers would forgive her sloppiness.

Now she approached Mik's writhing body and grabbed him by the arms. He was dead weight, even resisting her the best he could, but his misery did not help his situation; he was unable to fight her will. Rasia dragged him into the center of the pentagram and released him, then proceeded to plant a firm kick between his legs to keep him in place. He cried out, and his hands went immediately between his legs. He began to violently gag and wretch.

"Do you feel a bit, shall we say, violated, Mik?" Rasia looked down at him and shook her head in disgust. "It is a shame you are all heartless pigs, but I suppose that helps someone like me. How convenient that I will need the protection of the Powers for some time to come. Thank you for stepping up to the plate and becoming the very thing they desire."

Now she took the keys from the ignition and walked to the back of the vehicle. She opened the trunk and removed a massive hunting knife with a wicked jagged edge. After holding it up and admiring it in the moonlight, she returned to her drinking buddy, who was now lying on his side so the vomit could run freely out of his mouth. The Powers would enjoy that; it would be like icing on a slab of cake.

She laid the knife on the hood of the car and removed her clothing. Then, in the light of the headlamps, Rasia began her dance, the sacrificial dance, the dance which would summon the attention of the loving Powers. Once they gazed on her, she would ask their protection. Protection for all that was to come in her future and on her quest for The One.

She danced slowly at first, chanting with love. As she progressed, her movements became more and more charged, and the light began to reflect from beads of sweat that were forming on her chest and back. Mik lay on the ground squirming in his great pain. He was doubled up on his side in a fetal position, for he still could barely move. He could see her though, and the metallic taste of petrifying fear was filling his throat and mouth.

Now she was chanting so loudly she was nearly screaming. Her dancing body had become a blur, and Mik could not keep up with her with his eyes. She stopped suddenly and fell into a stony silence right next to him; she wanted him to see her. Rasia knelt beside him and smiled. She didn't say a word as she raised her arm, knife in hand, and drove its blade deep into his side, twisting it when it was in to the hilt.

Mik's body went stiff, his back arching violently. His eyes flew all the way open, as did his mouth, but no sound came out. Rasia removed the knife, but hardly a drop of blood came from the wound. It would not do. She grabbed his hair in her hand and pulled his head back, baring his neck, then she slit his throat, so deep that it lay wide open.

Now the blood poured out, even shooting onto her, and Rasia smiled. The Powers would be pleased with this. They would protect her as she made her offerings through life, and they would protect her as she sought The One.

She sat cross-legged on the ground next to Mik's twitching body, waiting for the confirmation of peace that the Powers would provide if they were pleased with her sacrifice. No sooner did the pig stop breathing than the peace came, and she stood, clear-headed and smiling. She hummed to herself as she used her own shirt to clean blood off her hands and face. Then she put on her jeans and a light sweater and climbed into the car.

As she started the vehicle's ignition, she wished her molester all the best. "Goodnight, Mikhail. Thank you for the help and information. Oh, yes, and for the wonderful time," she told him loudly as she drove off, honking her horn as she went.

R.W.K. Clark

CHAPTER 7

Corsica, France

The landing light on Flight 322 came on, signifying that it would be landing soon. The pilot began his gratuitous speech to the passengers as they fastened their seatbelts in preparation. Rasia finished her plastic cup full of cheap merlot and proceeded to hook her own belt safely together, the pilot's voice fading from her conscious as she did.

She had brushed her teeth thoroughly three different times since her encounter with Mik the night before in Kiev, but she swore she could still taste his blood. It wasn't altogether unpleasant; it was simply the thought of last night that she found so distasteful. For a fleeting moment, she wondered what happened to him after she left him bleeding on that gravel road, but she smiled and pushed the thought away. She didn't even care if he had bled to death out there. There was one less dirtbag in the world if he did.

The plane was descending fairly quickly now. Rasia closed her eyes and put her head against the headrest of her seat. She never had been a big fan of the landing; it was best to think on other things until it was over and she had her feet firmly planted on the ground.

When the landing was complete, she filed slowly out of the plane behind those in front of her. Her mind was not even there; she was thinking about the time she would spend in this beautiful country. She was excited to wine and dine, even though she would be doing it all alone. To be honest, Rasia Engres preferred to be alone most often. Others would never know and understand her as they did each other; Rasia was not like them, nor would she ever be.

France had been the perfect option.

The Figari-Sud Corse Airport welcomed as she disembarked. Once she got through the customs checkpoint and security, she followed the posted signs to the baggage claim area, and there she fetched her things before making her way to the car rental area. She had a reservation for an automobile; she hated using public transportation of any kind if she could help it.

Her car was a newer, and very comfortable one, which she immediately loaded with her bags. Once she was settled inside, she utilized the onboard GPS, typing in the address to the Residence Maria, the hotel she had booked. It would provide her with accommodations directly in the area where she would be doing her research. While it was not a five-star hotel, it was what she was looking for. It would be comfortable, and it would suffice.

The hotel was exactly what she had hoped for: the rooms were arranged in a 'bungalow' style, while all remaining connected. The landscape was lush, green, and quite beautiful. She admired it with a smile; beautiful flowers and foliage had always provided her with a level of peace, and she would need peace if she wanted her research to succeed. After all, she had only a week before she had to return to the University.

Rasia checked in and then followed the bellhop, with her luggage, to her room. After tipping him and shutting the door securely behind him, she took a look around. Queen-size bed, desk, television. Two nightstands flanked the bed, and each held a shaded brass lamp. The hotel offered no Internet service, so she intended to find out where the closest place was that would allow her to utilize theirs.

She realized she was ravenous, so she unpacked quickly and then took a hot shower. After fixing her hair, applying makeup, and dressing, she took the list of eateries that Mik had given her from her purse. Might as well start taking advantage of what the idiot had provided; after all, he had paid the price for it.

For her dining pleasure, she opted for a restaurant about thirteen miles from her hotel called The Kissing Pot. She ordered a glass of wine and pasta primavera, and she enjoyed a spectacular Nicoise salad beforehand. Everything was delicious, and she found herself more relaxed than she had been in months, if ever. After her meal she decided to take a seat in the bar and go over a bit of new literature she had brought with her to study in regard to her vampire quest; it was to provide a greater detail of true vampire history than anything she had ever had the pleasure of reading before, and she was excited.

"Hello," she greeted the bartender as she took a seat away from the other patrons. "I'd like a glass of nice Cabernet, please."

The bartender nodded and smiled in compliance. Rasia sat and pulled some books and her notebook from her bag. As she did, she pondered the 'vampire.' How would a human truly know one when they suspected it? What would be the signs? She had thought of these things countless times over the years, but she liked to revisit them. It was important to the discovery to make sure you had missed nothing along the way.

Her drink arrived, and she handed the bartender her credit card. "Please hold on to it; I will be having one or two more." He took the card and nodded once again, stepping politely away from her. Rasia opened the notebook to the first page and began to read her notes.

She was very deep in her thoughts. She would read and highlight a bit in her notebook, then make a written note of anything that had captured her attention. Much of what she read she had already learned; there was really nothing new in the beginning of this book, and this was one fact that drove her on in her quest. There was simply too much similar information throughout history for the suspicions of the existence of true vampires to be anything less than fact.

Rasia took a long drink of her Cabernet, breaking from her tasks to enjoy its taste and smell, just as a man of about thirty-three took a seat just two stools from her own. She looked at him out of the corner of her eye. He was blond and blue-eyed, sporting the 'pretty boy' look. He wore a suit jacket sans tie, along with matching trousers and good shoes. She made an effort to not look directly at him, and once she saw what she wanted to see, she turned her attention back to her wine and the books before her.

This did not deter him; he obviously had his eye on her before approaching.

"Hello," he began. "My name is Pierre Allard. I take it from an observation that you are a lover of good wine?" His voice was deep and rich, and he spoke in thick French.

Rasia glanced at him before taking another drink. Finally, she responded to him in French. "I am Rasia, and I do. Do you as well?"

Pierre breathed out a sigh, and his smile grew wider. "Rasia. It is a beautiful name. I prefer a stout cocktail, but one should never shirk a fine vino. Are you local?"

She looked directly at him for the first time. "No, I'm not. Are you?"

"Yes, yes. I was born and raised here. As a matter of fact, I am sure I will live here forever."

Rasia gave him a small smile before turning back to her own interests. She fished a pen from her bag and turned back to the front of the notebook, where her notes on vampires were kept. It would be best if this man took the hint; she had no time for him or his male shenanigans.

She could sense his movements, and he squirmed a bit for a moment. "Are you married?"

Now Rasia looked up and turned her stool so that she faced him directly. "I am not married. I am here on business, not for pleasure, and I am not interested in cheap one-night stands. If you do not fancy wasting your time, I suggest you try to hit on the brunette in the booth behind us with the gap in her teeth."

This statement evoked loud laughter from Pierre, and his eyes sparkled as he looked at her. "Regardless, would a chat with drinks throw a wrench in your plans?"

She considered his statement. No, it would hurt nothing, but she knew with certainty that he was interested in much more; they all were! She decided to indulge him, however, so she set her pen down, closed her book, and crossed her legs. "What would you like to chat about, Mr. Allard?"

His eyes scanned her face as if he was not at all sure what to make of her and her standoffish attitude. "I suppose whatever comes up. I was simply having a drink or two, and since you were alone I thought we could just… talk. If it's a problem…"

Rasia shook her head. "No, it's not," she said. "I'm simply not fond of being constantly approached for no apparent reason. You seem harmless. What do you do?"

Pierre was tracing the lip of his glass with his forefinger, watching himself as he did. "I have a number of interests in which I dabble. I have mostly invested in some clothing designers, and I provide them with financial backing, but there are other things I do to occupy my time. How about you?"

Should she be honest? Why not, after all, she had already told him her first name. "I am a journalism student at the University in Kiev."

"Ah! Journalism, how interesting. What do you want to do when you begin working?" He seemed friendly, and Rasia felt no physical pressure from him.

She took another drink of her wine and then signaled the bartender for another. "I will be entering an internship with a major paper there. Do you not have a day to day job?"

Pierre took a breath. "I do not need to work at regular employment."

So, Rasia thought. Here it comes. The bull and the lies that men use to impress a woman. The crap they tell you when they want to get down your pants. She could have a lot of fun with this guy. No better place to indulge her own distasteful habits without getting caught than... France.

"What does that mean, exactly?"

Now Pierre flashed Rasia his most charming smile. "Well, my father was killed in a plane crash five years ago, and he left my mother and me fairly well off. I would rather have him back though, I must say."

"Yes," Rasia replied. "So you focus on your investments?"

He simply nodded and turned his attention to his drink for a moment, the smile fading from his face. The bartender brought her a fresh drink, which she immediately took a drink of. She set it on the napkin, thinking hard. Her mind was beginning to turn already.

"So, Pierre, tell me about your youth then. Did you go to college?" She was no more interested in this man's life than she was in advanced chemistry, but she had some very intriguing thoughts about his money, that much was certain.

So, for the next hour, and another drink later for Rasia, she listened to the dashing Pierre Allard relate to her the 'tale' of his life. Most of what he related to her Rasia had the insight to realize was utterly false; ridiculous ramblings of an egotistical womanizer. She did, however, believe he had the money he so often managed to work into the conversation. He simply knew too much about investing to be blowing smoke in her direction regarding that aspect of the conversation.

He seemed to be thoroughly enjoying discussing himself, and so like any 'good' woman, she helped him stroke his ego by listening and pretending to be astounded by all that he said he was. She even went so far as to touch his arm and laugh hysterically at his stupid attempts at humor. How men disgusted her! Thank the gods she was a good actress. At least, she was when she wanted to be.

He was just wrapping up a story about an escapade that he had experienced while on safari in Africa, and even though Rasia held his eyes and smiled and nodded in all the right places, she barely heard a word he said. She was too busy planning and scheming within the confines of her own mind.

"So, Ishmael turned to me and said, 'At least she wasn't as big as that elephant!'" He roared with laughter, and Rasia followed suit. She allowed her own amusement to end early for the sake of ordering another glass. She had been counting his drinks, and he was on his fourth now, each were quite stiff. Rasia herself was just ordering her third, and he nodded for the bartender to bring him a fifth.

She smiled at him, making sure the grin touched her emerald eyes. "Too bad this place is so busy," she told him. "I would simply adore a moonlit walk along the Gravona River. Do you drive, Pierre?" Not only would she not allow him in her room or go to his quarters, wherever they may be, but she also would not be seen in her rental vehicle with this man. At least, not considering what she intended to do to him; he was going to have the time of his life, literally.

Now Pierre's eyes seemed to smolder, and his smile became more of a leer. He cast his eyes up and down her entire body, finally settling them on her face. "Yes, I drive. Would you like to take a ride to the Gravona? I would be more than happy to accompany you there. You will just love the atmosphere."

Without speaking, Rasia rose from her stool and began tucking her things into her bag. She smiled at Pierre as she motioned for the bartender to close out her tab, then she leaned against the back of her stool seductively. Pierre simply stood himself.

"I drive a fire red sports car. I will meet you out front, yes?" He threw a bill on the bar and motioned to the bartender with his eyes. "Keep the change," he muttered in the man's direction, then he focused his eyes back on hers. He was trying to see whether or not she was serious.

She held his gaze. "Absolutely. I will need just a moment here to gather my things, and I need to visit the powder room. I will see you in ten minutes?" Pierre nodded as she signed the slip handed to her by the bartender and then retrieved her card.

"I'll be waiting," he replied, and they went their separate ways. Good, Rasia thought. As far as anyone in the bar had seen, they left each other and went in different directions.

Rasia took her bag into the bathroom after gathering her books. She relieved herself and freshened up, then took an angora wrap from her bag and threw it over her shoulders; the night would likely have a chill. Soon, she was heading out of the bar toward the front door of the restaurant.

She figured she would have all sorts of fun tonight.

CHAPTER 8

The Gravona River was quite large, and much of the waterway led through woods and forest, though some were located in a well-lit area. It was a weeknight, and there were only a handful of people near the suspended walkway over the river, which was exactly where Pierre took Rasia for their riverside 'walk'.

The pair disembarked from his sickeningly high-priced vehicle, and Rasia allowed Pierre to take her by the elbow and guide her as they walked. He was obviously quite familiar with this area of the river. The breeze was fairly warm, and the night air was clean and refreshing. It had been a good choice to indulge herself in this place.

They found a bench which allowed them to sit and rest for a bit. Pierre produced a flask from the pocket inside his suit jacket and removed the cap, offering it to Rasia.

"What is it?" she asked him with a seductive smile.

He returned her grin eagerly. "Just a wonderful bit of smooth bourbon. Do you like bourbon?"

"Absolutely," she replied, and she took the flask from him and pretended to take a hearty swig of the liquid inside. "I do love a good taste of bourbon." She handed the flask back to him and gazed at him flirtatiously.

"Pierre," she began once again. "I want to tell you I have not been with a man in quite some time, and I adore making love outdoors, but there are still a few others here. Do you know of a place that is, should we say, a bit more private. I would still love to hear the rushing river, though." She winked at him.

Pierre's eyes lit up for the hundredth time that evening. "Hmmm. I would say I know some spots that would put us under cover of darkness while keeping us within earshot." He took her by the hand and stood. He certainly was getting a bit anxious to get her totally alone. "Follow me, Rasia."

She obliged. It was true that she had not been with a man in some time; the fact was she had never been with a man, and as far as she was concerned, she would keep it that way. Unless, of course, the payoff was greater than the sacrifice, and there was only one circumstance she would consider worthy. This man had nothing to offer her but the high she would feel as the life drained from his body.

They left the walkway and came to a slight groove in the grass along the river: a trail. They took this, and within minutes they came to a grassy clearing, where Pierre removed his suit coat and spread it over the ground. "Have a seat, Rasia. Here, take this flask. I need to excuse myself for one moment, my dear." He stepped off into the trees, into the darkness.

The sound of the river was quite loud; she knew this was the perfect spot to put this dog out of his misery. Oh, how good it would be! Granted, she had just taken out Mik, but that was a vengeance thing through and through. Rasia Engres had come to adore the feeling she got from a willing victim who had never done anything to harm her.

She removed her wrap, allowing it to blow in the wind along with her long locks. She posed purposefully, face to the sky and wind in her hair. It would be vital that he see her perfect profile in the moonlight; this would seal the deal. She was at the point where she wanted to see the fear and realization of death in his eyes more than anything else. To mess up now simply would not do.

She heard Pierre coming toward her through the twigs and bushes. She kept her eyes closed and lay back, supporting her weight with her elbows. "Oh, Pierre, dear. What has taken you so long?" Her French was perfect!

She heard him utter a low growl of desire. He lowered himself next to her, and she felt the palm of his hand cup her face at the cheek. She wanted to cringe; how men sickened her! She fought the urge and made herself lean into his touch.

In an instant, his lips were on her mouth. He tasted of alcohol, but his kisses, indeed, were sweet, to say the least. This man had practice, which was more than she could say for the idiots before him. Maybe this would be more difficult than she thought, but she highly doubted it. She certainly had the power to rid the planet of this... vulture!

She returned his kiss eagerly, but her avidity had nothing to do with lust or passion. She wanted him to fall into her grasp, and from his response, she could tell it was working wonderfully. She lifted her right hand and tangled her fingers in his blond hair, pulling slightly on it just for effect. Now she decided to pull out the bigger guns, and she arched her hips toward him, pressing herself against him as best as she could in the position they sat.

Pierre's hand found its way under her silk shirt and began to caress her nipple, making Rasia sick to her stomach. She pushed the feeling out of her mind with determination and moved her hand to his crotch and began to stroke him through his trousers. He moaned, and taking his hand from her breast, he began to fumble clumsily with the button on the pants.

Now was the time. She took her hand from his bulging penis and reached into her own back pocket, where she pulled out a medium-sized pocket knife; in a swift move, it was opened. With a single swoop of her arm, she drove the blade into his scrotum with an upward swinging motion. He didn't jerk away, he didn't even really move. All he did in response to the knife buried in his genital region was stop kissing her. He froze, a look of confusion on his face.

Rasia pulled upward once again on the handle while the blade was still deep in his flesh. She then pulled it out completely before re-planting it into the upper part of his inner thigh. She twisted it, looking him in the eye and smiling at his shock.

"You should be careful who you pick up in bars, Pierre Allard," she told him as she took the knife from his trembling body and wiped it on the jacket that lay beneath them both. Then she folded it and returned it to her pocket before she walked to the water's edge and began to clean the blood off of herself. He was going nowhere; she took her time.

When she returned, Pierre was still lying there, ghostly white and barely twitching. He would bleed out completely in a matter of moments. She began to dig through the pockets in the jacket and retrieved his wallet, which she placed in her other back pocket.

"I'm sure you don't mind contributing to my cause. A college girl like myself needs all the financial backing she can get," she said, but she realized he was already dead. After finding the keys to his sports car in his trouser pocket, she smiled with satisfaction and turned and walked away, leaving him hidden there behind the trees and shrubs.

Who knew when his body would be found?

∞

Rasia took the fire red Italian sports car, driving it while only after she had torn her wrap in two and used the pieces to cover her hands. She drove herself to a shopping center a few blocks from the Kissing Pot, and then parked the vehicle there, not bothering to lock it.

She left the keys in the ignition and the door open. Rasia expected the police to want to question her if she was still even in France when they found his body. It didn't matter; she felt completely safe. She quickly drove the fifteen-minute drive back to her hotel.

Back in her room, she looked the wallet over. According to his identification, his first name was actually Gerard, Pierre was an alias.

The wallet was loaded with cash money, which she put safely into her bag. She then took the wallet and placed it into the trash bin and, using crumpled paper for kindling, set fire to it. She sat up into the night, watching it burn with the window open and the fan on, then she flushed its remnants down the toilet.

All in a day's work.

CHAPTER 9

The morning greeted Rasia with a kiss from the sun as it shone through the window of her hotel room. She smiled to herself as she recalled the way the man's blood had felt as it ran through her fingers. Then she laughed at the money that was tucked into her bag. It had been a good night in more ways than one, and if things went her way, today would be even better.

She rose and called room service, ordering coffee, orange juice, and a couple of croissants before hopping into the shower. Afterward, she donned a sweater dress of gray and matched it with black suede knee-high boots. She added a black onyx and silver bracelet and earring set, let her hair hang in natural long curls, and applied light makeup. She finished just as her breakfast arrived.

Today she would visit local government offices and libraries to see if the region had any good information in books or microfiche on vampire history in the region. It was important to her to take advantage of the abundance of knowledge provided around the world. After all, whoever said that 'the vampire' would live or work in Ukraine? He could hail from, and live in, any place around the world. She would not limit her knowledge by being stubborn and ignorant.

∞

She left the hotel and drove her rental car to a city building which held records regarding the town's residents and their vital statistics, current, and past. She wanted any information that would simply catch her eye. She never truly knew what she was looking for, she only knew that she would recognize it when she saw it. Excited, she pulled up and parked the car, humming as she walked up the steps and into the main entrance.

A brunette with ridiculously long false eyelashes sat behind the main desk. Other official employees milled about, but none of them seemed to be aware that she had even entered. She approached the desk and placed her bag on it. "Excuse me," she began.

The woman, whose nametag read 'Monique,' looked up at her and smiled. "Bonjour."

Rasia returned the smile tightly. "I am conducting research for a magazine article and need to access public records from this region. Can you help me?"

Monique stood, grabbed a tablet and pen, and approached the desk. "What is it you are looking for?"

"I am not really sure. Mostly just local political family histories, I think," Rasia said.

The woman listened intently. "Any information we have is going to be very limited in this aspect, as we are currently computerized," Monique told her. "If you are looking for anything from even the near past, it would be best for you to visit our library."

Rasia persisted. "I will take any information you can give me, please."

Monique nodded curtly and smiled once more. "You may have a seat over there. It will take me about twenty minutes. I will find out if we can permit you to use our computers. Will you need me to print off the available information?"

Rasia nodded. "That would be wonderful if it is possible, thank you."

"There is a charge for each page printed. Will that do?" she asked.

Rasia nodded once again and turned to a small grouping of chairs arranged around a square center table. She sat and reached out for one of the magazines that were there for those waiting. She found herself more thankful with each passing moment here that she had studied French.

Monique returned after only a few minutes and roused Rasia from the article she was reading. "Excuse me, Miss," she said.

Rasia looked up and then glanced at her watch in surprise. "That was fast," she replied.

"Yes, madam, but unfortunately we have no public records here on anyone without being given a specific name," she said. "It is not possible to allow you to simply search our databases. If you could provide me with a specific name, I would be able to help. Otherwise, my hands are tied, I am sorry."

Rasia shook her head. "Are you sure?" Already her heart began to beat a bit faster.

"Yes" replied Monique. "Perhaps you could do some searching at the library, as I suggested, and then return if you narrow down what you are looking for. We really do need a name to be of any assistance to you."

"Well, I appreciate the help. I will be back if I get lucky, I guess," Rasia told her.

Monique turned and walked away, nearly leaving Rasia to her thoughts alone. She returned to her desk, and Rasia sat for only a moment wondering where she would even begin. Well, in the same place as always, she supposed; at the very start. She certainly would not waste her visit to the area by doing nothing at all. She would visit the libraries, begin reading local history and keep her eyes out for any of the red flags she had come to look for all the time.

"Well, thank you anyway. Where is the library located?" Rasia fumbled in her bag for her notebook, which she fished out along with a pen. Monique gave her simple directions; the library was only about six blocks away.

∞

Ten minutes later, Rasia was walking up the concrete steps of the public library, a renewed sense of hope. She was feeling a mixture of emotions.

She spoke to the librarian, telling her what she was looking for. She explained that she would like to search for local political families and their histories; all she wanted to do was write a simple article on the town. The librarian was able to easily assist her. She took her to a dusty back room which contained the town's archives: birth, marriage, death, and other vital records from as far back as the town was old.

"Not all records will be here, because the further back you go, the slimmer the chances of records even being kept becomes," the librarian stated. "If you need any assistance come get me. Do you know how to use the microfiche machine?" Rasia nodded absentmindedly. She was ready to dig in. "Very well, I will let you get to your research." The librarian left, letting the door close behind her.

There was a massive rectangular table in the center of the room which was surrounded by cabinets containing the town's records on microfiche. They were arranged in a very organized fashion, and Rasia was excited. This was a wealth of information; if only she knew what she was looking for, if a vampire or his family came from this general area at all, she would find the information here for sure.

After choosing a machine and arranging her things for use, she began to dig, but it would prove to be no easy task. She compared it to searching for a needle in a haystack, and it proved to be so. Rasia spent the entire afternoon on that specific day of her holiday searching and seeking.

Everyone was normal. Everyone was well known and local. She went into the archives back two-hundred years, and she came up empty-handed and frustrated. Finally, she threw up her hands; it was not to be today that she would stumble over her break. She would find it, though. She would not give up until she did.

But for now, she would get back to her life.

CHAPTER 10

The weather in Kiev was chilled and rainy when she returned, and she ended up back at her room at the University soaking wet and chilled to the bone. Her roommate had left for her own holiday, of course, and Rasia was relieved that she would have their room to herself for her own purposes. Once she had showered, she made a hot coffee and wrapped herself in a robe before sitting down to re-read the information she had gleaned at the public library in Bonifacio, hoping to find something, anything, that would set off a light in her mind.

She read and re-read, covering notes over and over again, and not just the ones she had taken in France. She read through her lifetime of notes in the lamplight of her room, drinking one stiff cup of coffee after another, but Rasia found nothing. She was frustrated, and she was exhausted.

But there was yet another thought: she had a mission. She did not want to waste time focusing on any specific city. She determined that she would not allow herself to get tunnel vision regarding anyone or any place in particular, so this temporary failure was a good thing, a blessing in disguise. After all, she had her studies to complete, and an internship at the Kiev Post that would begin at the end of her year. Those things could not be neglected. She had goals and very high aspirations, and no one could bring them to reality but she.

She would keep her eyes and ears open, and she would see how things panned out for the object of her obsession.

At the beautiful age of 23

Rasia graduated from the University at the very top of her class. She attended no year-end parties as commencement approached. Rather, she focused harder than ever on her studies. She would be going out on her own very, very soon, and though her 'vampire project,' as she had come to fondly refer to it in her own mind, was still in full swing, it was going very slowly.

Since returning from France, she had begun to refocus her attention back to her year-end studies and her pending internship at The Post. So preoccupied was she with her education and budding career that it was all she could do to just keep her antennas up, but she did so thoroughly. It seemed, however, that her investigation was at a standstill.

Her internship at the Post began smoothly, and within a month, she had a nice little flow going. While she was mostly just a 'gofer' for the real employees, she was always looking for and taking advantage of, opportunities to make herself and her presence known there. She was determined to be one of the finest reporters the paper had ever seen, and so she put a strong focus on the tasks at hand. If Rasia knew anything, she knew how to win.

For the next year, she put her nose to the grindstone. She excelled in all she put her hand to, for Rasia took nothing 'half-way.' She intended to become a crowning success in this life, with or without the success of the mission that had been handed down to her, but she was no quitter; she simply knew what to pay attention to and when.

Her internship lasted one year, and she was then immediately hired on as a legitimate reporter. Initially, she was given small assignments, and she used them to gain the recognition she deserved. It was during this time that her personal goals began to take on a new shade.

Rasia felt frustrated with the lowly position which she found herself in. She spent her nights contemplating her own life goals. What did she want? She wanted power. She wanted to be in control, and she was not. She knew what she had to do to gain it, but ultimately it would take time.

During the times that she held these thoughts, a rage would build inside of her. She was angry with her situation, her mother, her life. But then, in all honesty, Rasia knew that her entire life was dictated by anger, and she used it as fuel to fulfill her own selfish goals and desires, it just seemed to have worsened as of late. Professionally things were ideal, just where she wanted them, but she didn't care; she wanted things the way she wanted them, and she would have them that way.

She wanted to rule the world.

In efforts to channel this unrelenting fury, Rasia threw herself even deeper into her work, and even though the pieces she was writing for The Post were very basic in nature, she wrote them with excellence. Her boss loved her work, and her co-workers praised her, but the fact was they hated her, and she them, but nothing about other people mattered to Rasia Engres except what they could give her.

∞

Toward the end of her third year with The Post, Rasia decided, for the first time during her employment with the paper, that she would attend the yearly holiday celebration festivities the paper threw for its employees. She chose to go only because she had finally caught the editor's attention, and he had specifically mentioned in passing that he would see her there. Skipping out would not be an option this time.

The night of the party, she chose her clothing and her hairstyle carefully. She wanted to keep the attention she had finally earned, and Rasia was not above using her physical beauty to get a grip on another human being. She picked out a form-fitting red satin dress that came just to the middle of her thigh. With it, a diamond necklace, bracelet, and earrings, along with six-inch white satin stilettoes. She wore her hair up off her neck and let wisps of it fall around her face. She looked perfect.

When she arrived at the rented party venue,

everything was in full swing and cheer abounded, but Rasia felt nothing but anger at having to mingle with her co-workers. She allowed herself to feel the emotion, but she planted a friendly smile firmly on her face and toughed it out.

The bar was open, and she made a beeline directly to it. "I'd like a glass of wine, please," she informed the bartender, who nodded and turned to fetch her drink. She turned and cast her eyes over the festivities going on. So pathetic were these work-a-day dogs! Oh, well, whatever it took.

She felt a hand on her shoulder and turned sharply. The editor of The Post, Vitaly Orlov, stood there, smiling at her broadly. "It's good to see you here, Rasia. Are you enjoying the party?"

"Of course," she replied. "Who wouldn't enjoy such extravagance? You all really go all out."

He nodded and smiled as he looked around, eyes full of pride. "Yes. Working for this paper was always my dream, and I am proud of all that we do. Are you alone? I didn't see you with a date."

"Yes," Rasia said. "I am currently 'relationship free,' and I don't care much for one-night escorts."

Vitaly nodded. "I understand completely. Well, I need to make the rounds, but I am hoping to touch base with you again. Try to enjoy yourself, Rasia. I have gotten the impression that this type of affair is really not your thing, but our success depends on the strength of the team, does it not?"

She felt her blood begin to boil at his condescending

tone, but she reined in her response. "Absolutely, sir."

Vitaly nodded and walked away, smiling at all he made eye contact with. Soon he disappeared into the crowd completely. Rasia couldn't have been more relieved.

She turned and took her drink from the bar and took two quick gulps before stopping the bartender once again. "I'm going to need another before I get into the mix, please."

"Rasia Engres," came a strange voice from behind her. What was this, a conspiracy?

A young man of approximately her age stood smiling at her. "Do I know you?" she asked him.

"No," he replied. "I'm Demyan. Demyan Orlov, Vitaly's nephew. He has spoken of you often, and I recognize you from the photo they publish with your articles. It's nice to meet you." He took her hand and kissed it; all she could do was watch him with amazement; no one had ever dared to touch her before.

He had brown hair and blue eyes, and he wore a thin, but attractive, mustache. He was tall, attractive, and very polite. For a fleeting moment, Rasia considered what fun it would be to see what his liver looked like, but she quickly pushed the thought aside. This was her editor's nephew; he was off limits.

"You are a relation to Vitaly? Interesting," she began. After taking a sip of her wine, she asked, "Are you a writer, or do you work for the paper at all?"

Demyan laughed at this. "No, no, no! I wouldn't work for The Post, though Uncle Vitaly would love to have me. I am an attorney. I practice criminal law."

"Ah, noble profession," Rasia replied, and then she turned her attention back to the party. He was boring her now. Who really cared what this man did for a living.

But then it struck her: only moments after Vitaly had been speaking to her, asking about whether she had a date or not, this young man had appeared at her elbow. She was not psychic, but she could add two and two. Vitaly had sent his nephew over to meet her.

"Tell me, Demyan, did your uncle put you up to speaking with me?" She smiled playfully at the man, tilting her head flirtatiously for effect.

Demyan blushed slightly. "You are a quick one, Rasia Engres! Indeed he did. It seems I have had something of a minor crush on you for a short while, and he is aware of that," he said. "Please, don't be offended. Uncle Vitaly has a big heart. He is worse than a woman when it comes to playing the matchmaker."

"Would you like to walk around with me?" Rasia asked him suddenly. In the thirty seconds, since he began talking, she had clearly seen endless possibilities in her mind's eye. What kind of doors would open for her if she were to carefully date her editor's nephew?

Demyan's eyes grew wide with surprise, but he did not miss a beat. "I would love to," he said, and he crooked his elbow and offered it to her. She took it, and they advanced into the masses, drinks in hand.

Demyan's hands ran the length of Rasia's back as he kissed her neck. She was repulsed, but these things were necessary. She pressed her body against him and stared with boredom at the night sky over his shoulder.

He was growing very hard. It was time for her to put a kibosh on this, but she had to proceed with caution; she certainly didn't want to blow things before they had even begun. She could be very patient and calculating, but she wasn't about to give up her virginity. She was too skilled at manipulation for that. She put her hands on his shoulders and pushed him firmly, but slowly, away from her.

"Demyan, we need to stop," she began, making sure her voice sounded as though she was battling with the decision.

His breathing was ragged, and his eyes were clouded over when he finally looked at her as if he didn't really see her. "Why?" he asked. "Don't you want me?"

"Of course I do, my darling," she replied. "It's just that…" her voice trailed off.

A look of concern came over Demyan's face. "What, Rasia? What is it?"

Now she played him into her hands. She let her hands fall into her lap, and she looked at the floor. "Demyan, I am a virgin, and I am not ready for this yet." These were the only honest words Rasia Engres would ever speak to this kind, soft-hearted man.

His eyes lit up. "Oh, Rasia! I am patient." He wrapped his arms around her and embraced her. She buried her head in his shoulder for effect.

"You do not think me a prude?" she asked him.

He pulled back and looked into her eyes. "Never! I admire and respect this part of you!"

"Oh, Demyan, thank you!" She hugged him eagerly, rolling her eyes as she did. "Would you like to keep seeing me? I would like to get to know you better."

"Rasia Engres, there is nothing I would love more," he replied.

The stage was set. She had established yet another stepping stone to assist the upward trajectory of her professional life, but this one could not be toyed with too overtly. Rasia would have to tread very lightly with this one.

∞

The pair became an item quite easily, their relationship common knowledge among The Post's family. She was not surprised when Vitaly began to treat her as though she were his own daughter, and she used his affection for her to her advantage.

Six months into her fourth year with the post, she managed to hook what would prove to be one of the biggest stories of her career. It would launch her into the outer stratosphere as far as journalism was concerned, and it would prove to open much-needed doors for her in the future. It also proved to clear roads that would lead to everything she had ever wanted.

Anatoli Shevchenko was Prime Minister of Ukraine, and he was greatly loved by the entirety of the Ukrainian people. He was the catalyst that had changed the state of employment, as well as some of the issues the country had with poverty, and these points had ascended him to an idol status.

While Rasia had never paid attention to politics outside of what she needed to report, she managed to recognize a priceless story when she had her hands on one, and this one ended up being invaluable on several levels. Anatoli Shevchenko, a family man, married seventeen years and the father of two children, was having an affair with the daughter of one of his political backers. He was taking funds from the man and channeling them into an underground child slave circle which was catering to the deviant sexual needs of several politicians. These children were kidnapped from around the world and transported to the Ukraine, where they were held hostage until they were sold individually to a variety of pedophiles, many who owned several, and kept them for themselves. Both male and female children were falling victim to this ongoing, yet unknown, crime.

∞

Rasia had a petty argument with Demyan over her not wanting to attend a family dinner at his mother and father's home. There had been no yelling, but Demyan had tried to play upon her emotions by adopting the behavior of a young child, and Rasia found this to be deplorable. At a loss regarding how to deal with him, yet still refusing to attend, she had left his apartment with a promise to call him later that evening, and made her way to the corner tavern for a cocktail.

"A glass of Shiraz, please," she instructed the bartender as she took a seat at the bar. She removed her wrap and placed her bag on the bar, and as she made herself comfortable, she noticed a young blond woman two stools from her. The woman's eyes were red and teary, and though she made no sound, she was sobbing quite dramatically, gripping what appeared to be bourbon in her small hand.

The bartender brought her drink, and she passed him her credit card without a word. When he walked away, the reporter in her got the best of her, and even though she could care less what this waif of a girl was crying about, she asked. "Are you okay, my dear?"

The girl turned her head toward Rasia, sniffling pathetically. "No, not really."

Rasia let out a slight chuckle. "Obviously." She handed the girl a handkerchief from her bag. "Keep it. It looks like you need it more than I do."

She accepted it gratefully and proceeded to wipe her eyes and blow her nose loudly. Rasia smiled with amusement and took a long drink of her wine; momentarily the girl was forgotten. Rasia turned her focus to her cell phone.

"I hate men."

Surprised at the sudden words, Rasia turned to her. "Excuse me?"

She sniffled yet again. "I hate men."

"Do you want to talk about it? My name is Rasia if knowing my name will make you feel better," she said. "Sometimes it's a lot easier to tell our problems to a stranger."

The girl looked at her with red-rimmed eyes and smiled. "Yes, I suppose that's true. My name is Klarysa… Klarysa Klovel."

Immediately Rasia's radar went up. Klovel… Klovel. How did she know that name? Before the thought was even complete, it hit her: Dimitri Klovel was the head of the largest pharmaceutical company in the country, and he had a daughter named Klarysa.

Rasia decided it was best to pretend she had made no connection. "What's wrong, Klarysa? I am quite familiar with heartache myself."

"I don't know if I should talk to a stranger about it. I mean, it's sort of a big deal, but I need to get it off my chest so badly…" Her voice faded out as she broke into sobs once more.

Not wanting to push the girl, Rasia took another long drink from her wine glass and sat with her in silence. After a few moments, Klarysa pulled herself together. "I have a boyfriend."

"Yes?" Rasia replied. "I do too. We have something in common already."

Klarysa shook her head vigorously; the girl had obviously not mastered the art of interpersonal communication. "What I mean is, I have a boyfriend, but he is married, so I have to be very careful when speaking of him."

Now Rasia nodded. "I see the dilemma," she said. "But you can count on me, Klarysa. I will do no more than lend a shoulder to cry on."

The girl searched Rasia's face with her eyes, and when she was satisfied, she began to speak. "My boyfriend is a very important man. I would not be involved, but he is in business with my father, and my father pretty much gave me to him… as a gift."

Immediate hostility began to grow in the pit of Rasia's stomach, but she controlled herself. "And now you want out, yes?"

"No," Klarysa said. "I mean, yes, but not for the reasons you may be thinking."

Rasia waited patiently for her to continue. "You see, if I quit seeing him, it will enrage my father. My boyfriend does a lot of favors for him, and the other way around as well. But… I have discovered a secret."

Now Rasia's ears began to burn with curiosity. She knew in her soul that she was about to hear something big. "Who is your boyfriend, Klarysa?" she asked, her voice almost a whisper.

Klarysa looked around to make sure no one was eavesdropping. Then she leaned toward Rasia and whispered back, "Anatoli Shevchenko, the Prime Minister."

The revelation nearly knocked the wind out of Rasia, and it was all she could do to control her excitement and remain calm in appearance. "Have you been discovered by his wife?"

Klarysa looked around once again and, satisfied, she responded, "No, no. It is far worse than that…"

Now Rasia's curiosity swelled to incredible proportions. What could be worse than the Prime

Minister getting discovered having an affair? That alone would rock the reality of the entire country. It was indeed juicy stuff.

"Listen, Klarysa, if you want out of this relationship, I can help you, but you need to give me a good reason to get involved," Rasia whispered. "Let's move to a booth so no one can hear us talk, okay?"

The girl nodded, and both women stood and gathered their things. Rasia turned to the bartender. "Could you please bring us two more drinks and put them on my card?" He nodded, and she turned and followed Klarysa to a quiet booth located in a corner. Her cell phone rang as she sat. She looked at the screen only to see Demyan's name, so she silenced the phone. After that, she activated its voice recorder and laid it face down on the table in front of her. What Klarysa didn't know would not hurt her.

As soon as the bartender left them with their fresh beverages, Klarysa began to speak openly. "Yesterday I was at my father's vacation home with Anatoli," she began. "I was doing a bit of swimming, and I even had my personal masseuse come to give me a rubdown; I have been under much pressure."

Rasia nodded. "Go on," she said.

Klarysa paused, as if reconsidering, but finally she continued. "Anatoli left for a while to take care of some business, and after my masseuse left, I went up to our room to shower. When I got there, I saw some sheets of paper on the floor, as if he had dropped them on his way out."

Klarysa took a drink of her fresh bourbon, her face cringing from its bite. Rasia followed suit, keeping her eyes on the girl's face the entire time. Patience was the key now.

The girl took a deep breath and met Rasia's gaze. "I am so ashamed…" Her voice trailed off.

"Klarysa, tell me."

She looked as if she were bucking up, so Rasia gave her a few seconds. When she opened her mouth, the words came pouring out so fast she could not contain them. What she had to say was more than Rasia ever bargained for.

"I looked at the papers. I didn't mean harm, I was only going to put them on his desk, but on my way to it, some words caught my eye that just didn't seem… right," she said. "I saw names and ages, a list of them, very long. They were the names of children. I stopped and read the papers, and these children have been kidnapped and sold to customers of my father and supporters of my boyfriend." Klarysa started to cry again, so hard that she could barely breathe.

Rasia's heart was pounding. She reached into her bag and fetched another handkerchief for the sobbing girl. She then moved from her position across the table and sat next to Klarysa on her side of the booth. She wrapped her arm around her and pretended to comfort her, but she wanted the girl to stop crying; she had questions.

Once Klarysa calmed down a bit Rasia asked, "Do you have copies of these papers?"

"Copies?" Klarysa repeated. "No, I have the originals."

The girl reached into her own purse and withdrew an envelope, which she handed over to Rasia willingly. "They are being sold to these people for... for... sex!" She broke down once again.

Now Rasia looked around the room herself, then she opened the envelope and began to read the papers. After five minutes, she let the papers drop to her lap. "Klarysa, I can help you. I can expose this, and no one will ever know it came from you. Never."

It was too good to be true. Klarysa had not only dropped a bombshell of a story in her lap, but she had also supplied her with the proof. Rasia was not about to let this slip through her fingers. She would go to any lengths necessary to have this story. Any.

"Rasia, I do not think that is a good idea. It is too late for me. I belong to Anatoli, a mere piece of his property now. They will kill me, him and my father."

Rasia stared at the girl, her mind working a thousand miles an hour. "How will they know that you let the cat out of the bag, Klarysa?"

Now it was Klarysa's turn to be wary and confused. "Wait, how are you going to help me? Who are you and what do you do?"

Rasia chose her words carefully, but she didn't answer until she had the papers a safe distance from Klarysa's hands. She would not let the girl have them back. She would convince her to allow her to expose these men, these vile, vile men.

"Klarysa, I am a journalist with The Post," she began slowly, to not upset the girl. "I have connections, and I have ways to keep you safe. Come with me to my apartment, and we can talk about it privately."

Immediately Klarysa began to panic. She reached across Rasia's lap in an attempt to retrieve the papers, but Rasia grabbed her wrist and twisted it violently. Then, in a calm voice, she said, "Klarysa, think of the children. Now grab your things and walk out the door. I will follow you outside. If you do not cooperate, I will go to the police with the story and the evidence." Something in Rasia's tone must have convinced the girl, because she got her things together and stood, heading for the main door of the tavern. Rasia was right on her heels.

When they got out into the night air, Klarysa turned to Rasia. "Where are we going?" Her eyes were afraid. "I do not want to get hurt, I just wanted the right thing to be done."

"And I am going to see to it that it does," Rasia replied. "My car is just half a block away." She took Klarysa by the arm, sinking her nails into her flesh with just enough pressure to let her know she meant business. "We will go to a hotel, and there I will get the rest of the story from you. Then together we will discuss the best route to take, yes?" She didn't wait for the girl to answer. "I will see to it that no harm befalls you; if it does, it will be of your own doing."

In a few short minutes, the two were racing down the highway with Rasia behind the wheel. Now Klarysa must have been feeling a bit brave. "I am not going to let you do this. You tricked me when all I wanted to do was talk, and maybe listen to some good advice. I am not giving you permission to print this story. I will deny all of it!"

Rasia threw her head back and laughed as she shifted the gears of her car. "How will you deny it, Klarysa? I have the papers! The names of your father and the Prime Minister are all over them! You need to calm down. You are not thinking clearly."

Suddenly the girl began to weep quietly. She looked out the car window into the darkness, a forlorn expression across her face. She began to speak to Rasia in quiet tones.

"You do not understand what this will do to my life. Anatoli… my papa… they have done worse things to people who have done less to them. I am only property to them both, and they will dispose of me at will." Suddenly her car door flew open, and Klarysa leaped from the vehicle, which was speeding down the freeway at a very high rate of speed.

Rasia, however, didn't even flinch. The car door shut from the centrifugal force of the vehicle's movement. She looked in the rearview mirror just in time to see Klarysa's body bounce three times off the pavement, then it lay still.

Well, Rasia thought, it is her doing, just as I said.

She continued up the freeway. She would check into a hotel and call Vitaly. She would relate the story to him and tell him that two men abducted the girl as they tried to get into Rasia's car. Then, they were chasing Rasia out here on this road, and during the chase, she saw Klarysa's body eject from the vehicle behind her. The car then took the next exit and disappeared, but now Rasia was afraid for her own life.

Afraid indeed. The only thing Rasia was afraid of was failing to meet her own goals. Like she always said, she would go to absolutely any length to avoid that end. Any length.

R.W.K. Clark

CHAPTER 11

Rasia checked into a small inn about five kilometers outside of Kiev in the town of Telichka. The room was shabby and a bit grimy, but she would not be sleeping much while she was there. She parked her car in the shadows and cautiously took her bag into the room. She made sure the door was locked and bolted, and then placed a chair under the knob for even more protection. Once she was settled, she took her cell phone and rang Vitaly.

"'Hello, who is it please?" Vitaly had been sleeping, she could tell by his voice.

"Vitaly, it is Rasia."

He cleared his throat. "Rasia? I got a call from Demyan–"

"No, Vitaly. We cannot talk about that now. I need you to meet me. I have important information, information that will turn Ukraine on its ear." Rasia spoke in low tones to avoid any other guests hearing her.

Vitaly was still for only a moment. "Where are you?"

She thought for a moment, and then remembered that she had dialed his cell, not his home number. "I am at UA Hostel. Number 12. In Telichka. I need you to come now, Vitaly." She hung up the phone without so much as one more word.

Rasia stood and walked over to the window and peeked out of the curtain. The lot was still, no movements whatsoever. She sat back down on the bed and began to re-read the papers she had gotten from Klarysa, who was now roadkill.

For the next half-hour, Rasia read the papers over and over. They were the real deal; this was not a dream. The Prime Minister and the head of Klovel Pharma were involved in one of the biggest cover-ups and criminal rings in the history of Ukraine. This was a career maker.

A light knock sounded on the door, and Rasia jumped slightly. She stood and walked over to it, putting her mouth close to the jamb. "Vitaly?"

"Yes, it is I," came the response.

She removed the chair and opened the locks to her editor, who stepped into the tiny room, looking behind him as he came. "What is going on, Rasia?"

She occupied herself with locking back up and replacing the chair. Then she turned to Vitaly. "Sit."

He sat on command, never taking his eyes from her face. "Vitaly, I will begin by saying I could not go to dinner because I had a meeting at the tavern down from Demyan's apartment. It was confidential, so I could not tell him."

"Go on."

Rasia proceeded to relate the tale told to her by

Klarysa Klovel. As she got into detail, Vitaly's eyes grew wider and wider. At one point he even looked as if he may be sick. When she told him that Klarysa had been 'thrown' from the car of 'men' who had taken her, he looked panic-stricken.

"Rasia, we cannot pursue the story without proof or a verifying party! You called me here for this before you have even found witnesses to your accusations?" Vitaly rose as if to leave.

"I have records of some of the children, Vitaly. Official documents." Now she had his attention in full. He sat down hard on the bed, and Rasia pulled the papers from her bag and handed them to him. "See for yourself."

By the time Vitaly was finished, he had to excuse himself. He went into the small bathroom and shut the door; Rasia heard him vomiting in there. When he came out, he was flushed, yet pale at the same time.

"Some of the men, the buyers, on that list, are very prestigious, Rasia," Vitaly said.

She nodded. "Yes, Vitaly. This is a big one."

Both of them were silent for a couple of minutes. Then Vitaly spoke. "Since the girl was taken and you were followed part of the way here, I want you to find another room, maybe in a town ten or twelve kilometers from here even. Do you have your laptop? Can you work?"

"No. I have a full voice recording of Klovel's daughter on my cell, but that is the only technology I have on me," she replied.

Vitaly smiled and shook his head sadly. "A voice recording, too." Finally, he nodded. "Okay. You must get another room and call me from your cell as soon as you check in. I will see to it you get a computer. I need you to write the story immediately, and I need it in my email as soon as possible. You will stay in hiding until it goes to press and is released. We need to see what the immediate reaction of the public is; we need to know how these men are going to respond."

Now Vitaly stood and handed the papers back to Rasia. "Scan these and attach them to the email with the story. You also need to upload your recording and send that as well. When can I expect the piece?"

"Give me three hours after I have the computer. No problem," she said.

He nodded. "Okay. Go. Get the room." He dug a wad of cash out of his wallet and shoved it into her hands. "Use this, and don't leave a paper trail if you can help it. Be safe, and get in touch with me as soon as you can so we can get the ball rolling. I will be waiting for your call."

CHAPTER 12

The day Rasia's story was released in The Post, chaos broke loose, and Rasia Engres was very satisfied with the results.

Not only was Klovel taken into police custody for his involvement in the crimes he was accused of, but Anatoli Shevchenko, the Prime Minister, was visited by police as well. He barricaded himself in the bedroom of the vacation home and turned a handgun on himself, splattering his own brains against the wall and window. Countless records and documents were confiscated by authorities, who would investigate and attempt to track down as many of the enslaved children as they could locate. The entire country went into mourning; it was a situation which had no winners.

Except for Rasia Engres, who instantly became a national celebrity. She was promoted by Vitaly to hold the head position over a majority of her fellow journalists at the Post, which gave her the ability to get her grubby, devious mitts on the juiciest of stories. She doled out the light work to those beneath her, and she drove the other writers very, very hard.

She also was assigned her own photographer, a

lumbering young man by the name of Oleks. She insisted he accompany her almost everywhere she went; just the sight of the guy deterred the men who would letch after her on such a regular basis. It kept her in a secure position, able to avoid all of their advances easily.

Now she had her sites on Vitaly's position at the post. Next, she would aim to own the entire paper, no matter what it took. She was full of huge dreams and massive aspirations. She was enjoying her success, but to those outside of her personal world, she was uptight and unapproachable, cold even. Little did they know that 'fun' for Rasia was living in secrecy, minding her career, and looking for the mysterious person she so diligently sought.

So, for the next several years, those were the primary focuses of Rasia Engres. She covered high-profile stories for The Post with her cameraman Oleks in tow, and she wrote with an angry passion that kept her from going the distance and winning awards for her work. It was infuriating, and it drove her even more, to separate her writing from her emotions.

This anger she had bottled up inside of her was beyond her comprehension. While she didn't understand it, she continually tried to harness it and use it for her benefit. She would return to her upscale apartment whenever her workday was done, and she would study the witchcraft that was such a dominant part of her heritage, oftentimes practicing small spells alone. Her mother had continuously told her that this was a very dangerous thing to do. It was the combination of spirits and power that a coven provided which would keep a witch from crossing lines and boundaries, but Rasia didn't care.

She had even gone so far as to study up on this information. She found countless verifications in the pages of books which strongly recommended that a witch never, never cast alone. She pushed this advice out of her mind. The spells she did cast were so minor that they did little more than provide her with monetary and physical comfort on a consistent basis. What or who was she hurting?

With her real goal being to obtain earthly power and wealth for herself alone, she had no intention of ever welcoming another female, much less many, into her personal circle. Rasia Engres was not one to share anything. What she didn't realize was that her anger was a product of her private time activities; witching alone was making her eviler than she could possibly imagine.

She had no friends and no particular social circle. She participated in the social activities of The Post, such as parties and other festivities, only to save face with Vitaly and the rest on the paper's corporate level. They were pleased with her work, even though they encouraged her to keep her tone neutral. She had no intention of letting anything get out of control and ruin her plans to obtain power and success.

At the mature age of 28

Rasia was at the top of her game. She had not only Oleks firmly under her thumb but virtually the entire staff of The Post as well.

She didn't date, and outside of work, had basically no human interaction with anyone that really wasn't professional in essence. She was on her way, and nothing would stop her.

Rasia watched and listened quietly from a distance for any man from nowhere who would become one of the richest and most respected men in his country or even the world. She even kept her eyes out for women, but nothing set off her alarms. She simply kept the faith that she was meant to be the one to find the eternal life her kind so badly wanted and needed.

She must be patient until he or she gave themselves away. It was her hope they would do this sooner than later, but she would focus intently on the tasks before her and bide her time.

∞

In the summer of that year Rasia's own mother, Oksana Engres, was killed violently. She had become involved with some others who avidly practiced the craft, and while she had started the latest coven herself, she had become the envy of one particular woman named Vasilisa. She was younger than Oksana and had very high aspirations for herself in their coven.

Rasia was contacted on a rainy evening by one of her mother's closest friends and fellow coven members named Dina. The woman called her to inform her of her mother's death, fill her in on the details, and let her know that she was the next in line to receive the Book. Rasia, with her black heart and mind, was thrilled about the entire call. Not only would she have the precious

Book, but she would also no longer have her neglectful, love-starved mother walking the face of the Earth, and this was satisfying to her in every way imaginable. She hated the woman and her weaknesses. She had received her just deserts, as far as Rasia was concerned.

She received the call from her mother's friend Dina on a Thursday night. She had been working on a spell which would give her success in her quest for the true vampire, the one that could fulfill all the hopes and dreams she, and her ancestors before her, had ever had. The ringing of the telephone jolted her out of her focus and into reality.

"Hello!" Rasia yelled into the receiver, angry that she had been distracted by a telephone call.

The caller spoke in a soft voice. "Is this Rasia Engres?"

"Yes," Rasia snapped. "You have reached Ms. Engres. How can I help you? Who is speaking?"

"Rasia, this is Dina. I am the best friend of Oksana, your mother," the woman replied.

The response was enough to make Rasia even angrier. She had told Oksana on numerous occasions that she did not want bothersome calls. She had too much to worry about without thoughts of her in her mind.

"Whatever it is, I am sure she can help you better than I can. Now if you'll excuse…" she was immediately cut off.

The woman's tone sharpened greatly. "I am not one of your acquaintances, or even your enemy, girl, that you should use that tone with me!" Dina took control of the conversation immediately. The slight growl in her voice was enough to get Rasia to be still. "Your mother is dead."

This was met with silence on Rasia's part, but not due to shock. She was simply processing the woman's words.

Finally, she spoke. "What has happened, Dina?"

"The official cause of death is listed as an illness, but she has been killed by a younger coven member who sought to fill her shoes," Dina replied. "I am not calling you for friendly chatter. The Book is waiting for you to come to claim it. She will be put to rest in three days."

Now Rasia's curiosity got the best of her. "Who did this, and how was it done?"

Dina related the story of the young, ambitious coven member Vasilisa. She relayed to Rasia that Vasilisa had gotten into cahoots with two others, and together they had cast a spell that had caused Oksana to bleed to death after cutting herself, quite by accident, while peeling potatoes at her kitchen sink. The women had readily admitted what they had done to Dina and the others, voicing that Oksana was stuck in old traditions and rules that were holding the coven and its members back from their true potential.

"I loved your mother like a sister, Rasia," Dina told her. "I know there is no love lost for you, but you are entitled to the Book. I will not allow it to fall into evil hands, do you understand?"

Now Rasia became more talkative and inquisitive.

"Yes, yes, I'm sorry, Dina. The phone rang while I was working. Are you still operating with the coven?"

"No," she said. "I have made myself separate from them all. I will no longer cast or practice the craft in any way. It is time for me to go on with my life… quietly. When can you come? I want to put this behind me as quickly as possible."

Rasia told Dina she would be there the following evening, and then offered her condolences on the death of her best friend, Rasia's own mama. She hung up the phone gently and stared off into space. A plan was forming in her head, and it was ingenious.

The spell she had been working on was very detailed and very dangerous. A similar spell had been entered into the Book by her own grandmother, Rasia knew, but for it to work, a sacrifice of blood was required: one of their very own. That was why it had never been cast; for the most part, her ancestors were witches that tried to walk the straight and narrow, and no one in their circle would be considered for such a spell.

But Rasia was not only willing, she now saw this Vasilisa as a prime candidate for the bloodletting. A witch with a soul as black as her own? She would have the Book, which contained the original spell verbatim? Nothing could be more perfect!

Rasia picked up her telephone yet again and dialed the number for the airline she used for her travels. She booked a flight to her destination, which would take only two hours. She would leave at eleven in the morning. Then she called Vitaly and Oleks and let them know she would not return to The Post until the day after the next.

Now her success was guaranteed; not only would she have the priceless Book that was rightfully hers, but she also would not be forced to sidestep on the success spell by cutting corners or using substitutions, which was always dangerous. She would take every last drop of blood from this 'Vasilisa' and offer it to the Powers, and that would solidify her quest for the vampire in stone.

∞

By two o'clock in the afternoon the next day, Rasia was sitting at the home of her mama's dear friend Dina sipping a cup of mint tea and listening to all the morbid details of her mother's murder. Yes, it had been officially labeled a death due to illness, but that was how this Vasilisa and her minions had planned to do it, and for witches, this was a very simple thing. Now the woman had stepped up as the new leader of the coven, and the rest of the women, with Dina being the exception, had followed.

"I will step away from the group willingly and with no remorse," Dina said. "I am ashamed to be associated with such individuals in any way. It is best if you take the Book and go on with your own life, Rasia."

She nodded. "Where does this woman live, Dina?"

"She has the apartment downstairs from your mama's," she replied. "But it is my sincere hope that you let this go."

Rasia simply smiled. "I do not seek revenge for my mother's death. This woman obviously had her own motives, and those I do not understand, but it is not my business."

Dina stood and walked over to an old roll-top desk. She used a key to unlock it and soon produced the Book. She looked at it with love in her eyes and absently stroked its cover. "I cannot tell you how many spells your mother and I have cast together from this Book…"

She walked over to Rasia and placed it in her hands, but she did not let it go right away. "Do not use this for harm, Rasia. I know that you have a fury; your mother has often spoken to me about the hatred and anger within you, but this can turn all that around for you if you let it."

"You are familiar with its contents, then," she replied. "The only goal I have is to discover the true vampire and bring his power and eternal life to our kind. What is so wrong with that?"

Now Dina's eyes grew wide; she knew of the spell within that would accomplish what Rasia spoke of, yet she did not press the issue. Dina knew exactly what Rasia had in mind, and she would not interfere. Rasia was capable of inflicting pain, and that she knew full well. She would not become the sacrifice. Let Vasilisa pay that due if that was what Oksana's daughter had in mind.

"The woman works at the laundry on upper Kreschatyk Street. She is home by five-thirty in the evening," Dina said quietly before sitting back down and taking her teacup in her hands. "Do what you feel you must."

The two women finished their beverages in silence, and after another fifteen minutes, Rasia stood to leave, the Book in hand. "Thank you for keeping this safe for me. I will not be attending my mother's funeral. I could not do that with a clear conscience."

"That is if you have a conscience at all, Rasia," Dina replied quietly. She did not stand with her. "I hope there is mercy for your soul."

This made Rasia smile. She needed no one's mercy.

The daughter of Oksana smiled at her mother's friend, and without so much as a goodbye, she left the tiny house, leaving Dina seated in her rocker staring out the parlor window. Rasia had no need for the woman anymore. She had what she wanted and needed.

She got into her rental vehicle, a minivan with darkened windows. It would fulfill her purpose perfectly. She would take this woman Vasilisa and bind her like one had never been bound before. She would then drive back to Kiev with the woman in tow, and during the witching hour, she would sacrifice her to the Powers and do the casting that needed to be done. It was only a matter of time now until the real identity of the vampire was known.

Eternal life and power would belong to Rasia Engres at last.

CHAPTER 13

Rasia sat in the van just before sundown and watched the shabby brick building where her mother had lived, and where her mother's murderess still resided. She was less than a half-block away, and looked about as inconspicuous as she could, with a kerchief tied around her head and glasses with plain lenses on her face. She was sure her mama had shown a photo of her off to all the women in the coven. Oksana had been very proud of Rasia and all of her worldly accomplishments. She had really missed the boat with her misguided life, though.

Either way, if anything gave away Rasia's identity to this Vasilisa, it would be her hair; it was her most dominant physical trait. She would not be stupid enough to allow this woman to see her true appearance. With her plans set in stone, that just wouldn't do. No, it wouldn't do at all.

Next to her in the passenger seat was a bag containing handcuffs and zip ties, along with handkerchiefs and heavy duty duct tape. In the back of the van was a large box and a dolly, and on the inside pocket of her jacket was a capped syringe filled with liquid Seconal. She knew that this was going to be very, very easy. It was destiny, after all. It was the will of the Powers.

Just after sunset, she saw a blond woman shuffling toward the van from the direction the laundry was located. She had an oversized bag slung over her shoulder; her clothing was shabby, and her hair unkempt, pulled into a ponytail with messy wisps that had escaped from the band falling around her face. She looked dirty and tired.

Rasia watched as she drew near. She took the four concrete steps which led to the door of the apartments. There were only two in the tiny building, and of course, both were dark. A moment after the blond girl entered, a light came on in the main windows of the downstairs unit, apartment number one.

Rasia grabbed the bag from the seat next to her and slung it over her shoulder. She then popped the hatchback on the van; it needed to be ready for her. It wouldn't do to waste time, either. She would carry things out in a very calculating manner, according to the plan she had made.

She entered the building and stood for a moment, nostalgia washing over her like waves of nausea. Nothing here had changed, nothing at all. It was gray and dingy in the building and smelled of dust and mildew. Her mother had raised her in a hovel.

After only a minute's worth of reflection, Rasia turned her attention to the apartment with the number '1' written in black marker boldly on the door. As a child, it had been an actual '1', a gold-colored numeral held to the wood with screws. The place had gone downhill if that were possible. She took the syringe from her jacket and uncapped it, then held it down by her thigh and rapped sharply on the door.

It opened with a jerk. The blond girl stood there, an irritated look on her face. She sported dark circles under her blue eyes that made her look older than her years. She had taken her hair down, and it hung in greasy strands.

"Vasilisa?" Rasia asked.

She nodded. "Yes?" was her sharp, questioning reply.

Without hesitation Rasia raised her arm and swooped the needle down, embedding it in the girl's arm. She drove the plunger home, maintaining eye contact and smiling as she did it. At first, Vasilisa looked shocked, but then her eyes took on a knowing look, as though she had been expecting something like this.

Her knees buckled, her eyes closed, and she slumped to the floor.

Rasia took immediate action. She dragged the girl inside further and shut the door behind her. Opening her bag, she took out her supplies. She cuffed Vasilisa's hands behind her back and zip tied her ankles together. She then blindfolded and gagged her with the two handkerchiefs and then covered those with duct tape. Next, she went out to the van, retrieved the cardboard box and brought it into the apartment on the dolly, as if it were full and too heavy for her to carry.

Once inside, she laid the box, opened, on the floor and put it on its side against the wall. In a moment she had the balled up, soundly sleeping body of Vasilisa, the witch, nestled inside, and she taped the box securely shut. She loaded it onto the dolly and took it to the van. She used two wood slats to fashion a ramp for the dolly, and in no time she had the box shut up tightly and safely in the van.

Now for the drive back to Kiev.

∞

The first half of the trip was quiet. Rasia did not listen to the radio or make any more noise than she had to. She wasn't worried about waking the sleeping woman in the back of the van, rather, she was listening for any sounds that would signify that Vasilisa was coming to.

Into the third hour of the trip, she could hear the woman moving around, and soon she began to moan. It wasn't long before she attempted to scream but to no avail. When she ran out of breath and quieted, Rasia began to speak.

"I am Rasia Engres. The daughter of the woman whose position in the coven you usurped," she began.

She waited to hear the response, but she received nothing but silence from the back of the vehicle, so she continued. "So, you saw fit to blot out her life and attempt to fill her shoes, yes?" Still nothing, except for rapid breathing, and that she could barely hear.

"Are you familiar with the Book? Do you know the history of the women in my family? We have sought for generations now to obtain eternal life and power, and we have discovered the way," Rasia told her. "I can pursue my goals with difficulty or with ease. To do so with ease requires sacrifice."

Now there was kicking against the cardboard box, and Rasia could hear muffled moans. "It requires the bloodletting of a witch to secure that ease. You wanted recognition in the coven? Oh, my dear Vasilisa, now you shall have it!" This sparked laughter in Rasia, and soon she had to pull over on the side of the road, it overtook her so.

It was late, and there were no other vehicles around. They were on a dirt road with trees on either side. All at once, Rasia determined that this was as good a place as any. She popped the hatch and got out of the van. Once she had the door opened, she sat down next to the box, which seemed to be trembling from the fear of the female inside of it. Rasia patted it morbidly and looked into the starry sky.

"You should not have been so greedy, Vasilisa," she said. "Now, I will take you, box and all, into the woods, where I will prepare the Circle. You should be proud. What you will do tonight will change lives forever, dear one. You are quite valuable indeed."

Rasia arranged the makeshift ramp and removed the girl in the box. Then she fetched her bag, and taking a flashlight and securing it under her upper arm, she made her way carefully down a shallow ravine and between the trees into the woods.

After about three minutes of walking, Vasilisa began

to struggle a bit inside the box. She made noises as if she were trying to scream, so Rasia simply began humming loudly, enjoying the entire affair. Finally, she came to a bit of a clearing and put the dolly in an erect position.

"You may as well relax now, dear," she said. "I have to prepare the Circle. It's no good for you to work yourself up. You are doing a great service to our kind. I would expect that you would be honored, after all, not everyone has the opportunity to die for their craft."

She left the dolly and the box, setting her bag on the ground next to it. After gathering a bit of firewood, she built a small fire, just large enough to shed light around the clearing.

Then she moved the leaves that were scattered over the area and, retrieving a can of black spray paint from her bag, she drew the Circle and the pentagram. She then lit candles at each point.

Finally, she wheeled the box into the center and cut it apart at the corners with a utility knife. It fell apart around Vasilisa, whose eyes were filled with panic. She was covered with sweat, which Rasia knew the Powers would love.

She then got the Book from the bag and turned the pages until she came to her grandmother's personal entries. She scanned them over, making sure she had a firm grasp on her theories.

Then she took the spell she had written from her back pocket, where it was neatly folded.

With her utility knife in hand, she took her position

at the base of the pentagram and began to chant the spell in Latin:

"Quaerentibus vitam aeternam
Hic erit finis noster;
Devorabit timor
Ad hanc horam.

Terrae potestos, ventus, ignis, aqua,
Inducam ille qui vesco sanguinem in conspectus;
Ego dabo hoc holocaustum sanguinem et timor.
In reditum quia vestra promissum impleatur hoc nox!"

Vasilisa now began to squirm and struggle in full, for she understood her own demise would soon be a reality. Rasia repeated the spell in Latin once again, which translated meant:

"Eternal life will soon be ours;
Consume her fear this very hour.
Power of Earth, Wind, Fire, and Water.
Bring he who feeds on blood into sight.
I give this offering of blood and fear.
In return for your promise fulfilled this night!"

She continued to chant as she danced around the Circle. She had disrobed and was completely nude for the sake of the Powers, and as she danced, she began to sprinkle belladonna around the perimeter. After her fifth time around, she stopped suddenly at the base of the pentagram and turned to the witch in its midst. With great purpose and passion, she rapidly strode to her, and taking the utility knife firmly in her hand, she sliced the woman's throat with one deft swoop of her arm.

She then began to dance again, round and round, chanting over and over. The fire crackled and burned, and clouds rapidly filled the sky as Vasilisa's blood poured from her body and onto the box and the ground beneath her. All at once, the sky began to rumble and Rasia fell to her knees. A smile crossed her face, and she opened her eyes and looked to the sky.

The promise had been given. Soon she would know the identity of any vampire existing, and the power that gave him eternal life would become hers in full. She allowed herself to tremble as she gave thanks to the Powers.

Suddenly she rose and took lighter fluid and matches from her bag. Still naked, she entered the Circle and doused the now still body of Vasilisa with the fluid, then lit a match and held it to one of the corners of the box. With a loud 'Woosh!' the box and the witch on top of it were engulfed in flames.

Rasia turned away and began to dress. She grabbed her bag and the dolly and began to walk back to the rented van, the body of Vasilisa a distant memory in her mind already. She loaded the van and began to drive away, filled with twisted joy; it was only a matter of time now.

She hummed to herself, smiling, the entire drive back to Kiev.

R.W.K. Clark

CHAPTER 14

Rasia settled back into her routine of life and work as though nothing at all had taken place. So secure she was in the promise and her offering that she didn't even fret over it anymore. She had full confidence that the Powers would bring the bloodsucker to light. The promise would not have been made if he did not exist, so she knew that he was walking the Earth. All she had to do was wait patiently for his identity to be revealed to her.

So she threw herself into her profession vigorously. She didn't choose too many high-profile stories for herself because she wanted to be ready for the big one, for it was close to coming, she knew. Instead, she took the small ones and gave those that required travel or were of higher levels of importance to her subordinates. She kept Oleks with her at all times, unless they were off work, then she let him have time to himself. She wanted him ready when the time came.

In the meantime, she covered local pieces which involved crimes committed. She covered a series of Kiev murders which involved female college students. The story fed her bloodlust and thrilled her to her core.

That was the biggest she personally took on during that time, and it was extremely satisfying.

The murders began with a college freshman named Dasha Boiko. She was a journalism student, as Rasia had been. While Rasia was never moved by death, at least not in a negative way, she could relate to the girl because of her choice of study. She was also deeply disturbed by the manner in which the girl was killed: she had been beaten unrecognizable and sexually mutilated. Rasia had a deep hatred for anyone that abused women in this way. These facts are what motivated her to take the assignment herself.

She met with Vitaly to tell him of her intentions.

"Rasia, these types of stories seem to bring out both the best and worst in you," he told her after she informed him. "While you are tireless in gathering the facts, it is precisely this kind that you cannot seem to remain neutral on your writing and reporting."

Rasia sat across from her editor at his desk and smiled. "Vitaly, I think you know there is no way I will let a lesser journalist handle a job of such importance. As of now, they have no idea who had done this killing. What if one of our people, with less experience, were to come into contact with the murderer unaware? I will definitely take the assignment myself."

He looked at her in silence for a long moment. "I want to see any articles before you submit them to press, do you understand? There will be no personal interjections in the writing. Are we in agreement."

"Certainly, Vitaly," she replied. "I will be sure to

keep my personal opinions and emotions to myself."

He nodded and appeared to be satisfied. He knew that Rasia was a very driven woman, and he valued her commitment and work ethic. But he didn't want to cross her. He had gotten to know her fairly well since she broke the Shevchenko/Klovel scandal wide open, and he had a feeling she could be a bit treacherous if she wanted to. As a matter of fact, he had a feeling she would go to unmentionable lengths to accomplish the ends she desired.

"Fine, I trust you," he said. "Go ahead and get the main story, and do any necessary investigating you feel you need to, but be careful, please. I look forward to reading the piece."

Rasia left his office with a sense of smug satisfaction. She intended to not only investigate. If she had her way, she would find this person and cut off his most valuable parts before the law ever got to him. She swore this to herself with solid determination.

She approached Oleks at his desk. "We are going on assignment. We will be covering the University murder, so I need you on your toes. Meet me in the garage at the van, and don't forget all of your gear. Last time you cost us dearly with your irresponsibility."

"Yes, Ms. Engres," he replied. "I will pack up and be right behind you.

Within fifteen minutes, the two were in one of the vans belonging to The Post, and they were en route to the University. The girl had been found murdered in a patch of woods toward the edge of the property. Police would still be there investigating, and she wanted to at least have photos of the area, if not the exact spot itself.

When they arrived at the scene, officers were milling about, and crime scene tape was strewn around the perimeter of the area. Oleks was on top of his game; he began shooting photos while they were still walking. The man did have his good points, Rasia thought. Now, if only he weren't so damn stupid.

She put her thoughts about the photographer out of her mind and began to focus on the officers who were either standing or rushing around. No one had taken notice of her, as of yet. She didn't want to speak to anyone in uniform; she was looking for someone in a suit. Only they would be able to give her the information she was seeking.

She stopped walking and began to look more closely at the officers. On the other side of the crime scene tape, amid the trees, she saw a small group of suits, some standing, one kneeling. That was the man she wanted to talk to. A uniformed officer stood on her side of the tape, guarding the location and making sure that no one contaminated the scene. She activated the voice recorder on her smartphone and approached him.

Rasia pointed at the man on his knees. "Is that the lead investigator on this case?" she asked the officer.

"And who are you?" he asked in return. The name 'Melnyk' was on a gold plate which was pinned to the left breast of his uniform.

Rasia gave the man her best smile. "Officer Melnyk, my name is Rasia Engres. I am with the Kiev Post. I am here to get the story for our paper."

"Rasia Engres?" the young man's eyes lit up with excitement. "You did the story on the child slave scandal, yes?"

"Indeed, and I am going to do this one as well. Could you ask one of the men on the team if they could take a few moments to speak with me, please?" She continued to smile at him, even adding a bit of sexiness to her grin.

The young officer blushed a deep red and looked at the ground before saying, "Absolutely, Miss Engres. Give me just one moment please."

Rasia continued to flash her pearly whites and nodded at him. "Of course."

The officer walked away and stepped over the tape, approaching the group of suits on the other side. "Are you getting shots, Oleks? Make sure you don't stop for anything."

"Yes, ma'am." He was hitting his shutter button so fast Rasia was sure his finger would fall asleep. The thought made her laugh to herself.

The suit on his knees looked up at Officer Melnyk and listened to what he was saying. He then looked over his shoulder at Rasia before standing. He said something to the other investigators, then turned and walked up to her, his hand extended.

"Ms. Engres! Hello! I'm Detective Shevchuk, and I am the lead on this case," he began. "How can I help you today?"

Rasia shook his hand as he spoke, then responded.

"We are here to cover the story. I'm hoping you are willing to give me whatever information you are free to divulge and, of course, allow my photographer to get a couple of shots of the scene."

"I can allow him to shoot from there, but he may not cross the tape, as you know," he said. "Let's step over here and have a word privately."

The detective crossed the barrier, and he and Rasia stepped off to the side. "What do you know so far, Detective?" Rasia asked.

"It's a horrible crime," he said. "The victim was eighteen-year-old Dasha Boiko, a first-year journalism student here at the University. While we do not yet know the cause of death, I can tell you she was first beaten violently, which directly contributed to the death, we believe."

Rasia listened intently, glad her voice recorder was going in her pocket. She had a small notepad in her hand and made illegible chicken scratches on it for appearance sake. "She was only beaten?"

He shook his head and looked at the ground for a moment, pushing a small stone around with the toe of his right shoe. "No, no. There is more than that. Please be careful with your writing. We do not want people in a panic."

"Go on."

"Boiko was also raped and sexually mutilated in a ritualistic fashion," he said.

A confused look crossed Rasia's face. "What do you mean, 'ritualistic fashion'?"

"She was given a crude 'female circumcision' procedure, similar to those carried out in Africa. Her labia were removed with a sharp, rusty object, and it appears from the bleeding that this was done while she was alive." He took a handkerchief from his pocket and put it over his mouth, then wiped sweat from his forehead with it. "We can only hope she was unconscious when this was done."

Rasia's heart was pounding, and while she did not feel sick, she was on fire with anger. It took everything in her to contain it.

"You have no leads as to a suspect yet?" she asked in a hushed tone.

Shevchuk shook his head hopelessly. "No. None yet. That is really all I can give you right now, Ms. Engres. I do apologize. I must get back to the investigation."

"Thank you, Detective," Rasia said. She looked at the other detectives on the other side of the tape. They were all staring at her and Shevchuk. He turned and walked away.

"Oleks! That's all," she shouted at her photographer from where she stood. "Let's get back to The Post."

∞

Back at the paper, she sat at her desk staring at the wall. She had not started her piece yet; she was too busy obsessing on the murder and the nature of it to concentrate on her writing. She saw red; she had heard about female circumcision taking place in other parts of the world, but she had given them little more than a thought. They were not a part of her reality, and she had no feeling about them whatsoever.

Until now. Today she wanted to find this man, whoever he was, and she wanted to do to him what had been done to the poor Dasha Boiko. He was not a human being, he was a monster. She had nothing on him, even though she was a murderous and evil witch herself. This man had done this for his own pleasure, with no purpose. At least, none she could identify.

There was a knock on her office door, and Vitaly poked his head in. "How long have you been back from the scene?"

"Just about ten minutes. I haven't begun to write yet, and Oleks is developing," she replied.

He walked in and shut the door behind him. "What do you have?"

"Well," she began, "It's very limited at this point of course, but I'll tell you what I know." Vitaly sat in the leather chair across the desk from her and crossed his legs out in front of him. He waited as she chose her words.

"The killer beat the victim to death at the University's perimeter. He then cut her labia off with a rusty knife and raped her." She finally looked up at him and waited for his reaction to her bluntness.

Vitaly drew in a sharp breath. "Circumcision?"

Rasia nodded and held his wide-eyed stare. "I am going to investigate this case on my own. I will have my piece into you shortly and beginning tomorrow, I will investigate as I keep up with the progress of the police.

This is between you and me, Vitaly."

"Rasia, I can't have you running around playing detective! What if you put yourself in danger?" The look of concern on his face made him appear almost stricken.

Now Rasia busied herself with booting up her computer so she could write her story. "If you don't give me your support, even confidentially, I will do it in my free time, but I will be using Oleks."

"I will forbid him! I want you to do your job and no more!"

Now Rasia turned to her editor and gave him an evil, determined smile. She stared at him, challenging him with her eyes, and she said nothing. Vitaly read her look clearly.

Finally, he took a ragged breath. "Do what you must, but please carry a weapon, and I want no one to know what you are doing, Rasia."

"I am a weapon, Vitaly," she told him quietly, then she turned to her computer and began to write, dismissing him silently from her presence.

After a moment, Vitaly stood and, giving her one final look, left her office.

Not only would Rasia catch this animal, but she would also kill him herself, slowly and with satisfaction. Then she would present him to the Powers. They would be pleased.

R.W.K. Clark

CHAPTER 15

At five o'clock, the next morning, Rasia sat at her computer, a cup of steaming coffee sitting on the desk. She was browsing the Internet in search of crimes similar to the one committed yesterday, crimes where the perpetrator had never been caught. She found nothing even remotely similar, and it frustrated her.

This killer was fresh, and there was a very good likelihood that he would not re-offend. Maybe he just needed to get the fantasy out of his system. If this were the case, she would be paying someone on the inside to give her case details, or she would get nowhere. She would call Detective Shevchuk every day for information, of that much she was sure.

Next, she researched female circumcision. She had to learn as much about the procedure and ritual as she could. As she sat taking notes and browsing, the television was tuned in to the news and played in the background. She paid little attention until she heard the female commentator announcing the next segment.

"This morning we will be interviewing America's most loved winemaker, Cyril DeSai. DeSai has risen to god-like heights in the business world. He will be sharing the secrets of his success with us today, and he will also talk a bit about why American politics interests him so. All of this right after the commercial break."

Rasia literally dropped her pen. She stood, grabbing her coffee, and made her way to the loveseat in front of her set. Interested in American politics, was he? She was so excited she could barely contain herself.

She sat, her foot tapping on the floor, waiting for the commercials to finally come to an end. When the news came back on, it was a local spot before the international news returned, and the spot had nothing good to say.

"Another Kiev University student was found murdered late last night in her car in the parking lot of her dormitory. The first victim, identified as Dasha Boiko, was discovered in the woods surrounding the campus just over twenty-four hours ago. While the identity of this latest victim has not yet been released, investigators have said that her injuries suggest she was killed by the same perpetrator as Ms. Boiko. Stay tuned for updates on the case. Now, back to Alina Kolisnyk and the world-wide news."

Rasia was in shock for only a second. She quickly stood and pressed the 'record' button on her DVR, then grabbed her cell phone from her desk and dialed Oleks' number. "I need you to pick me up at my apartment fast. Another girl has been found from the University." She hung up without waiting for a response and went to her room to dress. She would have to watch the Cyril DeSai interview later; it was time to get moving.

"Oleks, this killer is binging," Rasia told her photographer as she climbed into his personal vehicle. The sun was just coming up; he had made good time. "We have a serial killer on our hands. I knew it!"

The photographer simply nodded. "Where to, Ms. Engres?"

"University," she replied. The police will be there, and I need to be there too. Do you have your camera?"

"All I have is my personal equipment," he said with apprehension. "I can photograph, but they won't be as good as if I had a full kit."

Rasia nodded. "No matter. Good enough. Now step on it; we have work to do. No driving like an old lady, now. We don't have time for that."

Oleks punched the gas, and they sped through the city streets in silence. Rasia was deep in thought, staring out the passenger window of the car. Who was doing this? Whoever it was, he had gone off the deep end. Without more information from the police, she had nothing to go on research-wise. She was going to have to come up with a solid plan if she was going to get her hands on this guy and have her way with him.

They drove around the University until they saw the lights flashing on the police vehicles, then they parked on the street and ran to the center of the action. She was running so fast that Oleks the oaf was having a difficult time keeping up with her.

They no sooner got to the lot than Rasia saw Detective Shevchuk standing next to the tape talking to a man she recognized as the coroner. The detective saw her out of the corner of his eye and turned to her, one hand held up.

"Give me a moment, Ms. Engres, and I will speak with you," he said.

Rasia stopped and nodded, catching her breath. Oleks finally caught up and doubled over to catch his breath. "You need to lay off the cookies and cakes if you are going to continue working for me, do you understand?"

He nodded as he panted, but he was unable to respond. "Now get it together so you can start shooting."

She took a few small steps toward the detective and then took her phone out and activated her recorder once again. After only about three minutes, he turned and walked toward her. He spoke in very hushed tones.

"As you have probably guessed, we have another victim," he said. "Same injuries. Guaranteed it is the same killer."

Rasia nodded. "It's serial. I knew it. There was no passion in the first killing. It was something he had obsessed on for some time," she said.

"Yes, and now we have to keep the rest of the girls here safe. The campus will probably go on lockdown." The detective looked exhausted. Dark bags were under his eyes, and he was pale.

Rasia treaded lightly. "Can you give me a name?"

"Yes, but that's all. We found identification in the vehicle she was found in, but she was unidentifiable," he shook his head in disgust. "We know it's her because her roommate verified that she never came back to the dorm after classes, or even took her evening meal. Her family has been contacted." Now he cleared his throat. "Tania Kushnir. Twenty. Third-year Liberal Arts."

Rasia looked at him with concern. "Do you need coffee? I would be happy to get some for you and your men, Detective." Now was the time for her to buddy up to this man; it would definitely pay off in the end.

His eyes lit up. "That would be wonderful. We have been here for hours."

"I'll bring them back, black with extras. I'll return shortly. How many?" She smiled comfortingly.

He shrugged a bit, a sad, exhausted look on his face. "Ten should do. Thank you, Ms. Engres."

"I think you should call me Rasia. I have a feeling we will be getting to know each other better, sir," she told him, then she abruptly turned and walked toward Oleks, who was shooting the parking lot and the crime scene from a little further back.

"Oleks, we are done here. Take me to the restaurant. These men need a bit of energy." Together the two ran for the coffee and quickly delivered it to the exhausted officers. They needed to get back to the office as quickly as they could; there was no time to waste. What the rest of the city saw as a horrible killing spree taking place, Rasia saw an opportunity, and there was no one better to jump as it presented itself.

"Irina, get me coffee right away, and get Vitaly in here as soon as possible," Rasia yelled at the receptionist as she passed by her. She entered her office and didn't even get the door shut before Vitaly came running in.

"I need you back at the college! There has been another - …" He got no more words out.

Rasia interrupted him. "I have already been there. Do you think you are working with an amateur?"

"You have been there?" He was surprised but pleased.

She nodded and took her seat at her desk. "I need that coffee, NOW!" She turned her gaze to her editor. "Of course," she told him with a snarl. "Tania Kushnir. Twenty years of age, Liberal Arts. Now if you have nothing better to do than doubt my abilities, I have a story to write. Excuse me."

He smiled and nodded as he backed out of her office. He shouldn't doubt her; she had been knocking his socks off for years. He would let her get her work done. She intimidated the heck out of him these days.

Rasia began to tap away fiercely on her keyboard, careful not to let any elements of emotion leak their way into her writing. She was not only going to cover this story, but she was also going to break the case and dole out the much-deserved justice this man had coming to him. If this were any other high-profile case, she would focus on submitting an award-winning piece, but now she only wanted him dead. Her anger was growing by leaps and bounds.

In less than thirty minutes, she was e-mailing the completed article to Vitaly. She called Oleks' extension, and soon he was in her office showing her his proofs. She chose appropriate photos and sent him to have them completed. "Get them to Vitaly yesterday," she told him with a sneer.

Now, she sat back at her desk and took a breath. She was considering what she would do next in her investigation when suddenly she remembered the interview with Cyril DeSai she had recorded at home. She jumped up and grabbed her bag and left her office, closing the door behind her.

"Oleks, I need you to take me home for my car, please," she said, and continued walking to the front of the building, the cameraman on her heels.

She was very anxious to hear what the winemaker had to say. She could hardly wait.

∞

Rasia sat down on her loveseat, a cup of coffee in her hand, and used the remote control to pull up the recording of the DeSai interview. In a few moments, it was up and running. The commentator with smiling blue eyes was making introductions, telling the people of Kiev that the next guest was a Frenchman who made wine and was now living as an American citizen.

"Cyril DeSai, welcome to our program. We are so happy to have you," she began. "Are you enjoying Kiev?"

The attractive man with long black hair and black eyes smiled at her. "It is amazing! I have wanted to visit for some time, but I am so busy these days."

"I'm glad you are enjoying it. Tell me, how long have you lived in the States?"

DeSai went into vague detail regarding his childhood in France, his history with fine wines, and his move to America. Rasia listened intently, her eyes glued to the television screen. He was charismatic, well-spoken, and extremely attractive. From the way he talked, she could tell he was highly intelligent, and it was no wonder his business was succeeding as it was.

Soon, the interviewer asked him about his involvement in American politics.

"I am only dabbling on the local level, in New York of course, and that is only at the urging of my friends and business associates," he said. "To date I am involved with the governor, advising him and assisting him with the current issues he is addressing."

The interviewer smiled flirtatiously. "Don't be coy, now, Mr. DeSai. Rumor has it that the governor considers you to be his right-hand man. He has even said you are the power behind the throne, so to speak."

DeSai laughed out loud. "I would not go so far as to say that," he replied. "The governor is a highly intelligent man who is more than capable when it comes to his position. Let's just say I offer him a listening ear."

Everything that was said after that was lost on Rasia. It was him; she knew it. She couldn't prove it yet, of course, but she knew, if she were right, this man would begin to quickly rise through the ranks. She squirmed in her seat and smiled. She would visit the States, and she would begin to investigate this Cyril DeSai for herself. She would also need to go to France once again; yes, that would have to come first.

She would discover the truths about this man soon enough.

R.W.K. Clark

CHAPTER 16

Over the next several weeks, Rasia's focus was divided between the murders and trying to keep an eye on her French-American target. He faded in and out of the news, and once again, she found him drifting to the back of her mind, but the killer was a busy boy indeed.

One week after the second victim was found, there was yet another. This one was discovered by a neighbor, her body sprawled and bloody in her apartment, the door left ajar by the murderous beast who had done her in. The same modus operandi, the same unrecognizable corpse. Kiev was in a panic. Even though the campus had discontinued classes after the discovery of Tania Kushnir, it had done nothing to stop the madness.

The third victim was named Nastia Hordiyenko. She was an 18-year old education major whose parents were putting her up in her own apartment to keep her safe and sound. It had done no good. She was beaten so badly that her left eye was embedded in her brain, the bones of the socket crushed over it.

Victim number four was another apartment dweller, and she was found in a park only four blocks from the apartment of number three. Lesia Romanyuk was a literature major hoping to teach high school. Her body was discovered under a bush with the same telltale injuries as the first three. This time there was a difference: splinters were found in her vaginal canal. The perpetrator had used a large branch from a nearby tree to violate the already dead young woman.

Police were at a complete loss. The murderer left no evidence behind. No hair, no prints, nothing. It was at this point that Rasia made a very rash decision: she was going to pose as a student and hang out in the area at night. She was going to show this person what it was like to be a real victim.

She planned to frequent the park. Only one victim had been found there, and it would be easy for her to park a vehicle a short distance away to help her make a quick escape. She would not be merciful to this man, not the way she had been with Vasilisa. Yes, she would use a vial of Seconal to subdue him, but what she would put him through would be nothing compared to Vasilisa's rapid demise. She could hardly wait to meet him, or for him to encounter her.

She did not know how long it would take her to capture his attention. She knew that his taste ran along the lines of the more innocent and demure. She would not wear alluring clothing or heavy makeup. She would carry a book bag with her tools in it rather than her regular bag, and she would wear her hair back in a ponytail. Blue jeans and a nice long-sleeved shirt would do, maybe with some simple stud earrings and a chain around her neck. She wanted him to notice her quickly.

Two days after she submitted an article regarding the fourth victim, she began her hunt. She rented a family-style minivan similar to the one she drove to her hometown when she fetched Vasilisa, and she parked it two short blocks from the park closest to where Tania Kushnir was found in the vehicle.

Just as she planned, she wore simple skinny jeans and a long-sleeved spandex top that was very modest in cut. She wore gold studs and a thin gold chain. She had gone shopping at a second-hand store earlier in the day where she purchased a vintage book bag, the kind with two metal clasps that held the bag's cover closed. She looked at her reflection in the mirror before she left her apartment: he would not be able to resist, and he would not know what hit him.

In her bag, she had a deathly-sharp pearl-handled straight razor and a metal 'fish' bat, the kind used to put fish out of their misery after being caught. She also had the obligatory handkerchiefs, tape, cuffs, and zip ties. Because he chose such hidden places to maim his victims, she was confident she would not be discovered while carrying out the work.

In her back pocket, she had the syringe full of Seconal, with just enough of the drug to knock him out while she bound him. She wanted him wide awake for his ordeal. In that way, he had shown more mercy to his victims. Rasia would not be so kind, no, and the very thought of him being awake nearly gave her an orgasm.

She parked the car she had rented and walked the short distance to the park very slowly. She wanted to get his attention. Thoughts crossed her mind such as what if he had decided to change his hunting grounds? No, she told herself, these vermin were creatures of habit. She might not encounter him tonight, but she would encounter him.

Rasia made it to the park and chose a bench only about one hundred or so feet from where the body of Tania Kushnir had been found in the vehicle. She took her syringe and uncapped it, carefully putting the cap into her bag. She then put her bag at her feet and removed a single Book from it: the Book that belonged to her family. She wouldn't even consider having another with her at a time like this.

For the next two hours, she sat patiently in the dark with only a single pole lamp lighting a small circle, and she was not in the light. She had the Book open in her lap to a chant of praise for the Powers, and she was humming as she whispered it into the night, a penlight in the hand that wasn't holding the syringe.

Suddenly she heard the snapping of a twig. She did not jerk in the direction of the sound, rather, she smiled. He was here. She knew it. It was hard to believe she would get lucky on this night, but luck had nothing to do with it. The Powers were blessing her for her deeds.

She began to chant a bit more loudly now, and after a minute, she could hear footsteps approaching from her left. Soon, a man was standing about eight feet from her. She looked up from the Book, then closed it and laid it on the bench next to her.

"Hello," she said calmly.

His voice was deep and nasty. "Why would you be out here this time of night?" he began. "Haven't you heard about the killings?"

Rasia smiled in the darkness. "Yes, but I am not afraid."

He continued to look at her in silence for a moment. He was short and stocky. He wore dark jeans and a flannel shirt along with a beret-type cap. She could not see his face, though his eyes seemed to be lit up in the darkness. He took a couple of steps toward her, and Rasia stood, the syringe in position in her hand. Her heart did not pound, and her breathing stayed calm. If anything, she felt like she was ready to eat a gourmet meal, not confront a killer.

"I assume you are the one," she said quietly.

He chuckled softly. "Did you have any doubt when you ventured here this night?"

She chuckled back. "You know so much less than you think you do."

Suddenly she ran at him full force, arm raised in the air, a growl escaping loudly from her lips. So surprised was he at her actions that he froze and put up his hands in a protective gesture. She leaped on him like a panther on its prey. A small cry flew from his mouth as he fell to the ground under her weight.

She buried the needle in his chest and sunk the plunger. He cried out a bit louder, but the sound dwindled within seconds.

"What have you done?" he asked her weakly.

She laughed out loud. "Wouldn't you like to know,

Monster?" Slowly he fell asleep.

Rasia acted fast. She retrieved the binding materials from her bag and in no time he was completely tied; only his eyes remained uncovered. Then she pulled rubber gloves from her back pockets and put them on. She dragged him into an area that was under the cover of bushes and trees, but yet had a bit of light from another pole lamp shining on it. Then she sat on the grass and waited.

Not twenty minutes later the pig woke. His eyes were confused at first, then he saw her and began to put up the fight of his life. She sat calmly and let him struggle until he was spent. As he lay panting, she spoke.

"You killed those girls, yes?"

His eyes narrowed, and she could tell he was smiling under the duct tape and kerchief. He made unintelligible sounds before he gave up and nodded vigorously.

"Ahhh. Does that turn you on, to treat these babies as if they are animals?"

He laughed with gusto through the gag, and Rasia shifted her position, getting on all fours. She crawled over to him, the sickness shining brightly in her own eyes. "Guess what, Monster? This is turning me on!"

His eyes grew wide, and his laughter grew still. Rasia fetched the straight razor from her book bag and opened it, letting the light from the lamp glisten off of its blade. Now the look in his eyes was one of sheer panic.

"You will bleed tonight, Monster. They will find you in the morning as they found the girls, and I will revel in the pleasure and satisfaction. That turns you on too, yes?"

Now he began to shake his head violently, the noises coming from him sounding much like "No, no, no," over and over and over again. She took the blade and cut his dark pants from him. Then she removed his underwear, then his shirt. He had lost his hat long ago.

He tried to fight her, but the lingering Seconal had weakened him way too much for his struggles to be effective. "Keep fighting; it assures me I am doing right. The Powers will bless me abundantly!" She giggled and cut through the last of the material of his shirt. He lay before her, bound and completely naked.

"Now I know why you kill. Do they all reject you, the women? You are fat, and you have a tiny dick," she said. You cannot get laid on your own, no?" Rasia stood and removed her own clothing for the Powers; he mistook her actions for interest, she saw it in his eyes. This pleased her to no end. She began to circle him and chant the Death Chant in a hushed tone, using Latin to summon the Powers.

She stopped at his feet. "You are to be a sacrifice to the Powers, Fat Boy," she told him, then she straddled his bound legs and sat upon them and took his penis in her hand. It was becoming erect. Good, all the better, she thought. The pain would be greater.

She held his member in a vertical position and considered. Then she spoke to him while holding it, looking directly into his eyes. "Should I lop it off in one quick slice, or should I saw at it a bit, hmmm?"

He tried to kick, but her weight kept him from it. "Okay, fine. I'll saw a bit!" She put the blade against his rapidly deflating penis and began. It was so sharp that it took only a couple of swipes, and suddenly she held it in her hand. Blood spurted from the empty spot.

"Oh, look what I have done!" she said with pride. "Not too much blood, though. I hope your little raisin balls give off more."

He was crying like a baby now, and this covered her with a warm tingly sensation. She took both of his testicles in her hand and lopped them off quickly. The slice caused the man to pass out.

She laid his package on his stomach and began to dance around him and continue her chant. She was able to repeat her praises several times before his eyes fluttered open and immediately filled with intense pain and fright.

"This is what you did to them. You took their lives, and you reveled in it. You never thought you would meet the likes of me though, did you Monster?"

He was weak from the loss of blood and barely made a sound in response. She walked to her bag, electricity shooting through her body. The Powers were pleased, indeed. She took the fish bat from her bag and turned to him.

"I forgot something," she told him, kneeling down, so he got a clear view of her crotch. "I wanted to tell you that these lips will never be taken by you like trophies, Monster. No, I will take from you instead."

She raised the bat over her head, and his eyes grew

wide as he understood what was about to happen. She brought the bat down forcefully onto his face and head so many times she could not count. Blood spattered onto her, but she didn't care, she had on gloves, and she had a trench coat in the vehicle.

She stopped only when she saw that his head looked like ground up beef. Now he was as unrecognizable as his victims had been. She smiled with satisfaction and looked into the sky.

"For you," she told the Powers.

Rasia bagged up all of her equipment after she made sure his heart was no longer beating. She dressed and covered her head in the extra kerchief that was still in the bag. Then she walked in a leisurely fashion back to the car. She unlocked it, put the bloody gloves in the bag and put on the trench coat, then drove off into the night.

She did not get a mile away before she pulled over on a bridge and pulled a pre-paid cellular phone from her bag and dialed the police. "A man is laying bleeding in Shevchenko Park, right in the middle, in the bushes," she said into the phone.

"Who is this? Where are you calling from please?" She hung up quickly and threw the phone into the river. She needed to get home, clean up, and get Oleks to pick her up and take her to the scene as soon as word came on the news.

She had never felt so satisfied in her life; now she could concentrate soon on a quick return trip to France. She was anxious to learn about Cyril DeSai.

Rasia was all clean and spiffy, and she sat before her television, coffee in hand, waiting in the darkness of her living room for the story to break. Oddly, the news was not announced until nearly six the next morning, and then it was only mentioned briefly. She calmly called Oleks and told him to fetch her with his gear, then she went outside to wait on him.

"Rasia," Detective Shevchuk said as she approached. "It looks as if our murderer may have been killed. Or else our murderer changed his strategy entirely to throw us off."

She forced herself to look confused. "What do you mean, Detective?"

"Well, we have a man here, dead, genitals removed and placed on his stomach. He has been beaten, but his killer tied him up well. His identification says he is Pavlo Zhuk. My men have ran his name, and he has an extensive history of violent and sexual crimes against women, but he has always slipped through the cracks." For the first time since Rasia met the detective, he was smiling. "I don't want to say officially, but off the record, I believe this is our man."

Rasia was jotting her chicken scratches in the notebook, her recorder running in her pocket. The only thing she needed was the man's name. She knew the rest, and she would take care to leave it all out of her story. Except for the pertinent information, anyway.

"What a relief. I knew it would all come to light. I will advise the girls from the college to continue to proceed with caution. Thank you for your help and kindness." Shevchuk stated.

Rasia smiled at him with a genuine smile and turned to Oleks. "Did you get a couple of photos?"

"Yes, Ms. Engres," he replied.

She nodded curtly at the photographer. "Good, Oleks. Let's go to The Post."

R.W.K. Clark

CHAPTER 17

After the solving of the University murders, Rasia was able to refocus her attention on Cyril DeSai on a solid basis, finally, and it proved to be perfect timing. Suddenly, DeSai was popping up in the news everywhere for his involvement in American politics. Now he was doing far more than 'assisting' the governor; he was rubbing shoulders with the American president himself.

The first thing Rasia did was catch a flight back to France, to the same area she had visited on holiday just years before. She knew she had felt drawn there, and she knew now that it was much more than a coincidence that she had chosen that area to research years ago, even though she had come up empty-handed.

She booked into her hotel just after lunch, then made the short drive in the rental car to the government offices. The same woman, Monique, sat at the desk. She had put on about twenty pounds and had dark circles under her eyes, but she still sported those ridiculously long lashes. Probably she has married, Rasia thought. That always makes one fat.

Now, she gave Monique the name: Cyril DeSai. He

had said he was from this area, so there should be no problem with the woman recovering the precious records on him and his family. She left with the name written on a paper in her hand, but she was soon back.

"There is no record of Cyril DeSai, or any DeSais for that matter, in this area, madam," Monique told her.

Now Rasia's heart skipped a beat. The man had lied and on national news! She gave the woman a simple thank you and went back to her car. It was time to head back to the library with the little information she already had on him. If he had any true history in the area, she would find it there.

This was what she currently knew: Cyril Gerard DeSai, Owner and Operator of Cliffside Wines, New York, United States. Unmarried; no known children and no current relationship. According to Mr. DeSai, he came to the United States just twenty years ago and established his vineyards and winery. Since then it has enjoyed astronomical success.

He had given a number of interviews, both on the local and national level. It had only been in recent months that a couple of the national interviews, which were given on early morning American news programs, had somehow found their way to television and magazines overseas. The odd thing was that since this had happened, the obscure man had gained a loyal fan base everywhere. Whether it was because of his smoldering good looks or his riches, no one knew, but the public's 'crush' on him seemed to be contagious.

She looked up from her notebook. Was this why she

was so intrigued by him? His magnetic personality? No, Rasia did not get 'crushes.' There was something about the man, she simply couldn't put her finger on it. He commanded the attention that no typical businessman would be getting, and he had lied; something was not right.

She sat for a moment in her vehicle and turned to the back half of her notebook. Here, she had taken notes on some other individuals who she thought may be vampires. James Gideon, an American who actually lived in Kiev and operated a chain of large department stores. He was rich and fairly attractive. He would prowl the city all night long and had a history of taking a variety of lovers, one of whom came up missing after her very first encounter with him. The man had been arrested, and Rasia had followed the trial as she investigated him. Alas, he was released on bond, and an old flame of the missing girl had shot him dead in the street. She crossed him off her list.

Roberto Hernandez, a Mexican drug lord who operated under the guise of the hotel owner. There were a couple of reasons this man caught her attention. First, there was a very strong rumor circulating that the handsome man drank the blood of young maidens in order to maintain his youthful appearance. Second, he had been arrested twice, and both times managed to escape his captors inexplicably. During his last escape, however, he had murdered a man who was working with the police to bring him down. Not only that, he had murdered the man's children and wife as well, raping her as she lay dying. When he was finally caught the courts sentenced him to death, and that order was carried out expeditiously. She had been forced to put a line through his name as well.

There had been a small handful more over the years, but none of them panned out proof-wise. All of them began to show their age eventually, and the time always came that their power or their popularity dwindled. A true vampire coming into his own should be on the upward rise; he would not want in his gains.

Finally, Rasia pulled her car from the curb and made the short trip to the local library. A younger woman was in attendance there, but Rasia already knew the drill, and in no time she found herself alone in the microfiche room, her belongings spread out in an orderly fashion before her. She was ready to get down to business, and she found she was more excited about her search than she ever had been thus far in her life.

If DeSai's family originated here, it had to have been long, long ago. So where had he really been born, and where had he lived prior to relocating to the States? Had his family really made wines, or was this just a cover for the suspicious man?

After two hours of skimming microfiche and digging, her shoulders and neck ached, and her eyes began to burn. She stood and paced the room for a bit, then resumed her task. That was when she got lucky.

She was skimming some information regarding a winery that had gone under a couple of hundred years prior. The reasons at first were vague, and she was making it a point to find out as much as she could, just in case DeSai's family had originally had a different surname than what he had provided everyone with, perhaps a derivative. One article was detailing the owner's life, and it happened to mention that his ventures in the winemaking business had begun with his own grandfather, who had gotten his start as a hired hand for a winemaker named DeSai in the 16th century.

Rasia drew in a sharp breath. Now she was on to something. Her heart skipped a beat as she took note of the man's name from the article, as well as the name of his failed winery. Progress, at last.

Armed with that information, she was able to find microfiche on that particular man, his winery, and his family background. Another couple of hours passed which consisted of locating specific microfiche, skimming, and taking more notes. By three o'clock, Rasia felt as though she was going blind. She was so thankful that no one else had come into the area to distract her.

After a brisk walk around the block, she got a second wind and headed back to the research area. She did a bit more digging, and within ten minutes of returning, she found the vintner's ancestor's information, and it led her directly to records on the historic DeSai winery.

She discovered a bit more than she bargained for, and she was not quite sure how to take any of it.

Adrien Geroux was the name of the failed winemaker's forefather. According to the records, he began as a laborer for another winemaker with the surname DeSai. Initially, Rasia could find no more information on the DeSai fellow, no first name, no family information, nothing.

Then Rasia struck a bit of gold.

She followed a thin lead regarding this 'Adrien,' and by utter accident, she came across his overseer's first name.

It was Cyril.

Rasia broke out in goosebumps all over her body, but not because she was unsettled. No, she was excited. She took the information and managed to track down the name of the ancient winery, and found quite a bit of valuable information.

The winemaker Cyril DeSai had run a very successful vineyard and winery four hundred years prior. He had a wife and two small children, and he was well respected in the community. His wine operation was quite major for the times.

Four-hundred years prior!

According to the records, however, he suddenly disappeared, with no trace of himself left behind. When workers came in one morning, they found the body of one of DeSai's right-hand men on the property's border, and further investigation on their part led them to the bodies of his wife and children.

DeSai himself was nowhere to be found.

Rasia could not take notes fast enough, and once she had exhausted all the information available to her in the microfiche room, which did not go much further, she sat back and reflected on all her discoveries.

Cyril DeSai had been a winemaker in the region literally hundreds of years ago. Was this the current DeSai's forefather? It had to be. But then what family line did this man come from? It clearly appeared that the first DeSai's family line ended violently and abruptly at his homestead on that one mysterious night. This led Rasia to two differing conclusions.

Either the Cyril DeSai of today was a fraud who had taken up this moniker to appear more authentic to his craft, or he was indeed her vampire.

She could barely contain her excitement. She did not want to get her hopes up too far; more than likely the man had simply changed his name, but why? Was he a criminal who was avoiding prosecution for some crime he had committed here in France? Was he a complete and utter con man who enjoyed good wine and knew how to make it? As she thought she wrote, as it helped her to keep her thoughts in order.

Finally, Rasia stood and began to organize and bag up her things. She could not come to a definitive conclusion with the information she had, but she could certainly arm herself with it and continue to look for the truth. One thing she could say for sure, her grandmother had been onto something very legitimate when it came to her vampire theories.

Rasia was just the one to prove them.

She left the library with a bit more pep to her step. She would take this information and go back to Kiev on the next flight. She would keep a very close eye indeed on the comings and goings of this man Cyril DeSai, America's favorite winemaker.

∞

The President of the United States was wrapping up his second term in office, which is all he was permitted to fulfill. Now a rumor was surfacing that he was recommending a nomination for DeSai to fill his shoes. What was so wrong with this? The fact that DeSai was not a natural American citizen. American law dictated that their president must be natural born, and Cyril DeSai was known to have been born and raised in France. The strangest part was that not a single American was bringing up this fact. They all seemed to worship him, even going so far as to melt in his presence.

At this point, Rasia had several notebooks on the man filled with research notes and information, and she had come to the solid conclusion that the Powers had fulfilled their promise: they had revealed the only vampire walking the face of the Earth. All she had to do was verify this and take the necessary steps to infiltrate his life. She knew this would not be as difficult as it sounded, but she had to meet him, and possibly get to know him first.

The world was getting to know him much better, however, and that included Rasia. He loved women. While he was not married, he had a different beautiful woman on his arm at every public appearance. This was one thing playing in her favor. She had never had any problem getting the attention of the opposite sex, all she needed was the right opportunity.

So, in order for her to confirm her suspicions on a more solid basis, Rasia began to stalk the winemaker, so to speak. She would keep her ears and eyes fixed on him and on his activities, at times even going so far as to jet with Oleks to wherever the man was at the current time. She always did this under the pretense of covering a particular story in whatever location he was in because it simply wouldn't do to have her cameraman asking questions or voicing wonder. Then, she would wait until she had time away from Oleks and go to whatever event DeSai was attending. This gave her ample opportunity to monitor him and those around him.

A true vampire would hold those around him in a trance, this she knew. She believed in her own power to resist him, even though she had never met him face to face, but those who 'followed' him at any given time seemed more than hypnotized by his presence. They seemed to literally worship him, and that included the politicians and the common folk alike. He never made demands; he never had to. It seemed that his wish was the command of anyone around him. Rasia found herself wondering how many of these people he had bitten and made one of his own. Little did she know the extent of truth that her ideas and theories held.

American politics was regulated by very specific rules. Sure, there were slight deviations and manipulations on the part of the people, but mostly the rules were abided by, at least in the view of the American people and the rest of the world, but when this particular man entered the political realm, it seemed that all of the rules went right out the window. Corners were not cut, they were eliminated entirely. He was wielding control over the people that they knew absolutely nothing about, nor were they suspicious of it.

On one of her undercover missions, she visited Cliffside Wineries in full disguise. She knew it would be very risky, especially if her suspicions about DeSai were correct, but she didn't worry. Her sacrifice of Mik to the Powers all those years ago would protect her from being discovered by the man for her true motives. Even a vampire would not be able to detect her presence if the Powers did not allow it, and they had given her peace.

She was too close to her dreams now. This was during the period that he was preparing to get not only his foot but his entire body, into the cracked door of the presidency. She doubted he would even be present at the facilities, but if she was going to pursue him and extensive information about him personally, she needed to at least visit his place of business.

So, she altered her appearance meticulously and took one of the tours that went on at the winery daily. She was amidst a group of other tourists, and though she doubted she would even catch a subtle glimpse of him, it gave her a prime opportunity to hear the opinions of the common people regarding this brand new American Hero.

The topic of the various conversations between the other tourists ranged from DeSai's striking good looks to his astounding rise in power. No one ever said a cross or negative word about him, rather, he was abundantly praised by all, and this alone was enough to make her smile, and her heart beat with satisfaction.

One such conversation, which she overheard in the lush cafeteria/restaurant at the winery, where the tourists took a lunch break during their visit, consisted of the fact that people seemed to be dying rapidly at young ages, more often than ever before in history. This concerned no one, surprisingly. They seemed to speak as if the world were a better place without the 'weak.' These words sent chills of pleasure throughout her entire body.

Oh, how her grandmother would be proud. With the help of the Powers, she had done it! She had really done it! Now, all that was left to do was to impose herself upon his life and steal what was rightfully hers: life eternal, and she would indeed do it.

She did get a chance to briefly see Cyril DeSai that day, much to her surprise. While eating a salad in the cafeteria and listening to the guppies speak all around her, he and his entourage came in for their lunch. He was surrounded, the gazes of adoration of all those in his company obvious. This sickened her; such worship should belong to her and her alone. Soon enough it would.

She was unable to view him for long. His party retreated to an inner room to dine, and they were quickly followed by servants wearing formal uniforms and carrying crisp linens over their arms. She did get to see him though, and the momentary event made her more determined than ever.

When she and Oleks returned to Kiev after that particular visit to the States, she began to research the deaths that were being discussed at the winery tour. She was curious whether they were natural, accidental, or murderous in nature. It was easy enough for her to compare the statistics: in the last several months, since Cyril DeSai had begun to rub shoulders with the American powers-that-be, the number of deaths had indeed risen alarmingly among the young. Most of them had pre-existing conditions consisting of everything from diabetes to addiction to mental illness. Indeed, the count had skyrocketed. What Rasia found to be curious is that it seemed that no one had taken notice of the deaths, and no one seemed to care.

There were no newspaper or magazine stories about the rise in the young death rates. There were no news or talk show broadcasts, no interviews with physicians allowing them to voice their opinions about the enigma. It was simply accepted by the entire world as commonplace. She also discovered that the phenomenon seemed to be radiating outward, with the United States being the central hub of the puzzle.

But she realized it was not truly a puzzle, not to her and not to the rest of the world. There was no confusion in America because that was the way America wanted it: get rid of the poor, and the potent will rise. It was what Rasia considered a natural result of an eternal vampire coming into power.

Yes, she had found him. Yes, she had proven his

existence to herself, and in only one solitary year from the time that he first gave the television interview on the worldwide news, the same morning she heard about the second mutilation murder. My, my, Cyril DeSai didn't waste any time now, did he?

∞

The very next morning, she sat at her office desk, the computer booted, a steaming hot mug of coffee on the desk before her. She had handed out the day's assignments to her underlings, including Oleks, whom she had sent to photograph the groundbreaking of a park in Kiev. She had sent him with a young, inexperienced male reporter who needed a bit of guidance. She trusted Oleks with the task if nothing else. She would spend the day expanding the amount of information she was gathering on DeSai.

A knock on her office door took her attention away from the screen. "Enter," she said loudly.

Vitaly walked into her office, a broad smile on his face. "Good morning, Rasia. I hope your trip to the States was enjoyable and fulfilling."

"Yes, Vitaly, thank you for asking," she replied. "How can I help you?"

He sat heavily in the leather chair across from her. "Something very, very significant has happened in the American political realm, and I need you to cover it to the fullest of your ability."

Rasia already knew though she was not aware of details. This was about Cyril DeSai, of course. He was going to step into the shoes of President of the United

States. How, she did not know, but she would find out.

"Cyril DeSai, the New York winemaker, is preparing to be sworn in tomorrow night as the US president," he began.

Rasia nodded, a satisfied smile playing at her lips. "Yes," she replied.

Now Vitaly nodded happily; he was quite energized by the facts, and she took note of it mentally. "He was not nominated, and for the first time in the history of the country's democracy, there will be no election. Somehow the businessman has been… appointed."

The smile never left his face as he spoke. He seemed to be hypnotized by the man without being anywhere near him. This amused Rasia to no end.

"I take it you are DeSai's biggest fan, Vitaly?" It sounded as though she was teasing him, but nothing was further from the truth. She was fishing.

He pulled himself out of his dreamy state and looked her in the eye. "Indeed. I think it is the best thing for America, and quite possibly the entire world, don't you?"

"Yes, I must agree, but I am sure that my reasons are my own," she said.

He stood and said, "Well, whatever the case for you personally, he will be sworn in tomorrow night, and there will be an inaugural ball as usual. All will be held at the White House. I have secured press passes for you and Oleks, so you will both attend the press conference that will be held after his swearing in. Any problems?"

Rasia flashed him a genuine smile of pleasure.

"Absolutely none. When will we leave?"

"Tomorrow morning. Your flight will depart at three in the morning. That will give you plenty of time to check into your hotel and get yourselves ready." Vitaly was beside himself, and she didn't blame him. This news would indeed change the world as they knew it.

But only Rasia knew the true extent of that change. In the end, she would be the one doing the changing, but for now, she was satisfied to let DeSai do the manual labor in her stead. She would not put up a fuss about it.

"Bring me the orders, and we will be on the flight," she told Vitaly. "Oh, and thank you for assigning this story to me."

He smiled at her. "Of course, Rasia. I would never consider sending anyone but my very best to cover a story of this magnitude." His smile was admiring and complementary. He left the office walking on air.

Oh, DeSai's power was tangible. She tingled from head to toe, embracing the joy that the Powers had given her. She was coming into her own, both for her and for those before her.

It was obviously meant to be.

R.W.K. Clark

CHAPTER 18

Oleks returned to the office and brought Rasia the proofs on the shots he had taken of the groundbreaking. His work seemed to be improving incredibly, and she was happy about this; he would do just fine for the trip. She had her doubts, but she was sure he would be fine. After all, her motives were far different from those The Post had. Yes, Oleks would suffice.

"Have a seat, Oleks," she said to him. He obediently took a chair and put his hands submissively in his lap. "We will be flying back to the States in the wee hours of the morning, you and me. It seems that the winemaker DeSai is going to be sworn into the position of the American president, and we will be covering the press conference."

The photographer nodded. "When does our flight leave?"

"We take off at three in the morning, so why don't you pick me up at my place at midnight," she replied. "We will need to be there early, of course, and it is just after noon now. We will both go home, take naps, and pack, whatever you need to do, yes?"

He nodded yet again. "Absolutely, Ms. Engres. So I will be out in front of your apartment tonight. I should leave now?"

"Yes. Go ahead. I will see you tonight, and don't forget all of your camera equipment, Oleks," she told him sternly.

"Of course," he said. "See you later on, then." He left her office, and Rasia quickly gathered her things to leave herself.

She had much to do. Not only did she need to choose an extraordinary outfit and make sure she opted for only the most attractive of accessories, but she also needed to make sure she was protected. She knew that DeSai held a passionate fondness for beautiful women, and she was one of the most beautiful; this was not bragging, it was fact. He also had the power to entrance. Whether it be with his mind or his eyes, she did not know. What she did know was that she needed to remain neutral in her being; she could not allow him any control over her or her mind whatsoever. Not if her plan was going to play out as she desired, and it had to.

There could be absolutely no deviation. She would have to present a completely detached affect if she was going to lure this particular fish. He was a slippery fish indeed, and it wouldn't do to have him break the line once she had hooked him, but it would take patience and calculation if she were to succeed.

She left her office and walked to the parking garage, where she got into her vehicle and locked the doors. She drove the short journey home smiling and humming to herself. Rasia could hardly believe that all her years of searching and studying were about to pay off. She didn't know how it was going to end, but she did know it would end to her benefit and in her favor.

Once in her apartment, she poured a glass of Cabernet and showered. She then packed her bag, careful to choose her most attractive outfit and accompanying jewelry. Once she had all of her things together and waiting by the front door, she took her wine and walked into her dining room, where she moved the table and chairs into the living area. She would need the convenience of her hardwood floor this evening.

She took a white piece of chalk and carefully and lovingly drew the Circle on the floor, then took brand new candles from the hall closet. She put one at every point of the pentagram, as is required by the Powers. Tonight she would implore them to grant her protection against the wiles of one Cyril DeSai.

Next, she made herself something light to eat, white fish, asparagus, and a bit of wild rice. She dined in the living room in front of the television, its channel tuned into the world news. She gleaned an abundance of information on DeSai's pending inauguration, and she noted that the male announcer spoke with glassed over eyes and a dim smile plastered to his face. He spoke excitedly of the new American president to be and gushed over how the future of the entire world was now so much brighter than ever before.

Rasia was sickened by how everyone had been

seemingly transformed into DeSai's puppy dogs almost overnight. She was certain that the only reason this had not happened to her was that she was a witch. The very same Powers that cared for her were protecting her and paving the road to success on this life mission.

Soon, she would take control. She would dictate and demand. She could begin to focus less on taking over The Post and focus more on ruling the puppets that DeSai had created. Even if she had to do so as 'the power behind the throne,' she would do it. But she was determined to not sleep with the man, not if she could help it, and certainly not right away. She had not protected her female essence for her entire life just to throw it at some self-indulgent vampire as soon as he told her she was beautiful.

No, she would use it as a weapon, and she would do it with a cunning manipulation that he had never known. If there was anything, she had it was power over men. Of course, DeSai was not just any man, but he was still a man.

When the sun went down, Rasia stood in the dining room, blinds drawn, and lit the candles on the floor. She finally removed her bathrobe and knelt at the base of the Circle, eyes closed, arms outstretched. She had the Book next to her on the floor, open to the most powerful spell of protection it contained. She began her chanting in a deep still voice, and soon, she was not even conscious of her own chanting.

Rasia and the Powers became one, and she stood and danced around the Circle with love and passion.

She threw her entire heart into her spell, not only asking for the protection of the Powers but also praising them for all that they had given her.

Time flew as she made love to the Powers, and soon she awoke naked on the dining room floor, the candles flickering and struggling to stay alive. The Powers had granted her request so certainly that she had fallen into a peaceful sleep. She looked at the clock on the wall; it was ten-thirty. Time to get ready to leave for the airport. Oleks would be there at midnight.

She rose and blew out the candles, contentment, gratitude, and peace flowing through her body. She went to her room and dressed in comfortable jeans and a sweatshirt, then she pulled her mass of long red hair back into a ponytail. She neglected any makeup, for she didn't need it to fly, and besides, it was packed already. Then she went and packed a light snack for the flight and put it into her carry-on bag.

Her cell phone had a full charge, so she dropped it into her purse and made sure that her charger was packed. She loaded her laptop and notebooks into her shoulder bag, and then looked at the clock. A quarter to midnight; Oleks would get here a bit early. It was time to head downstairs.

Just as she suspected, the young man was parked under the front awning. The doorman put her bags into his trunk, and the two ventured off for the airport, where Oleks dropped her at the main entrance and put his car on the long-term parking lot. He came jogging up to her carrying a single suitcase and his camera equipment case. They were ready to check their bags and get to the right dock. It was almost time for Rasia Engres to speak to Cyril DeSai face to face for the very first time.

She could barely contain herself, but true to her own character, contain herself she did.

∞

"Ladies and gentlemen, please turn off all devices and fasten your seatbelts. We will be landing at Ronald Reagan Washington National Airport now," the pilot said over the intercom. "Thank you for flying with us. We hope to serve you again soon."

Rasia and Oleks busied themselves with fastening their belts, and the photographer, who had been quite still most of the trip, finally spoke to her. "Are you as excited about interviewing Mr. DeSai as I am about taking his picture?"

Rasia turned to him and smiled, watching him closely. "Oleks! I did not know that you too were a fan of the famous winemaker!"

"What's not to admire?" he asked. "He makes wonderful wine, he is a success at business, the ladies love him, and now he will rule the most powerful country on Earth!" Oleks got a dreamy look in his eyes and leaned his head against his headrest.

Rasia said, "Well, that's fine, but remember who you are working for. You keep your focus on me, and we will be just fine. Admire the man from afar, will you?"

"Yes, Ms. Engres, of course," he quickly replied. "I would never compromise my loyalties."

The plane was descending, and soon they found themselves filing off with all the other passengers. They retrieved the bags they had checked and then made their way to the airport's rental car depot, where they fetched the vehicle Vitaly had reserved for them. From there, they drove to the Hotel and checked in. It was time to catch a nap, clean up, and get ready for the press conference that would take place that night.

But Rasia found that she couldn't sleep at all. She tossed and turned with excitement. She was anxious to initiate contact with the President-to-be, even if it was on an official basis. Finally, she gave up on sleeping and began to prepare the questions she would ask him.

She sat at the desk in her hotel room and wrote down several questions off the top of her head, then began to choose what she would ask by importance. She did not intend to make it easy on him, as she knew the other reporters would do. They would only be interested in stroking the man's ego, but Rasia intended to challenge him completely. Where was he from? How did he come to this position from nothing? He should answer these, but she knew he would not. She was more interested in his reaction than his response.

The conference was scheduled to begin directly after his swearing-in; selected members of the press were invited to attend, Rasia included. The inauguration and ball were to begin at seven in the evening, and it was now five-thirty. Time to dress.

Rasia wore emerald green satin which had been transformed into one of the most stunning yet simple dresses she had ever owned. It complimented her eyes perfectly, and she allowed her long red curls to hang loosely down her back, which she did not often do when wearing her professional hat.

With the dress, she wore emerald and gold earrings and a thin gold chain with an emerald and diamond pendant. She wore low-heeled black shoes embellished with green stones, and she sprayed her signature scent, lightly over her upper chest and wrists. She looked at herself in the full-length mirror. She was completely stunning.

Next, she took her cell phone and a tablet of paper with pen and placed them in her shoulder bag. That would be all she needed. Her voice recorder would be running, and she would jot notes like usual. She was getting more and more excited with each passing minute. Finally, she called Oleks. 'It is time," she said simply, and ten minutes later, they met at the hotel entrance and walked to their car.

This was the first night of the rest of her life.

∞

Rasia floated through the inauguration and the ball as though they were nothing but time fillers. She had no intention of drinking or getting loose; she was not here to party or celebrate, she was here to initiate changes, period. It seemed like the press conference would never begin, but soon enough, it was time for the members of the press to make their way into the designated room and take places of their choosing. Rasia and Oleks sat in the rear; subtlety was always best.

It wasn't long before Cyril DeSai entered the room and took his place at the microphones. He was incredible looking, Rasia had to admit it, even more so than on television, or even what she remembered from the winery tour. She did not want to look at him, because his appearance was alluring.

He opened his speech with the gratuitous words one would expect to hear from a newly sworn-in President. He would serve openly and only look out for the best interest of the American people, blah, blah, blah. Rasia fought back a yawn; his words were obligatory, and she was bored to tears because of this knowledge. After what seemed like ages, the new president finally welcomed questions from the press.

The first question was extremely superficial, and Rasia would have bet it was fed to the reporter who asked it. "President DeSai, will you be relocating from Cliffside to take up residence at the White House?" DeSai responded simply by saying he would be fully moved into the presidential home by the following day.

The next question came from a mousy female toward the front who asked him who would take over the business at Cliffside Wineries in his stead. "I have chosen Martin Steenway of Atomic Technologies," replied the President. "He is a brilliant businessman who has personal experience with winemaking; I have tasted his private products, and they impressed me to the point that I knew he was best for the job. I am also confident that he will do things at Cliffside the way I would want them done."

Rasia stood and lifted her hand, signifying she had a question. She caught the attention of Cyril DeSai immediately, his eyes almost clouding over and his smile fading. He immediately motioned toward her.

"Yes, dear. You in the back," he said to her, his smile quickly returning.

Rasia gave him a stiff smile in return, but she had to avert her own eyes from his. His stare was most potent, drawing one in almost immediately, and she was sharply aware of it. It made her a bit dizzy, and she found herself calling silently on the Powers. Finally, she said, "President, are you also confident that your experience running a winery qualifies you to run a country?"

DeSai continued to smile but completely side-stepped her question. "What is your name, my dear?"

"Rasia Engres," she replied, averting his gaze. "I am with the Kiev Post. I hail from Ukraine, sir."

He was looking at her as though she were lunch, she noticed smugly. Yes, the ball was certainly rolling, of that she was sure. After a brief pause, he answered her question.

"I am not only confident in my own abilities, Miss Engres," he began, "But I have full faith in the knowledge and abilities of my many advisors. This will be a team effort."

He was lying through his teeth, dazzling with his words, and Rasia knew this. She sat, pretending to be satisfied with the response, and the other members of the press began vying to be called on next. DeSai turned his attention to them, but Rasia caught his gaze several more times before the evening wrapped up.

The line was cast, of that much Rasia was certain. She needed to tread lightly though. This man was either very charismatic or very powerful, and she was certain it was the latter. She wanted, and intended, to maintain a safe emotional distance, but this one solitary meeting had left her with some doubts regarding her ability to do this. It had made Rasia's knees weak to hear his voice, and his eyes almost hypnotized. She would need the Powers to fill her with strength if she was to pull that off.

R.W.K. Clark

CHAPTER 19

Rasia and Oleks returned to their hotel directly after the conference. Oleks had wanted to stay, but Rasia had insisted: they were not there to 'party,' they were there to get the story. They retired to their separate rooms; they had a plane to catch back to Kiev at nine in the morning. She needed to sleep.

The day after she arrived back in Kiev, she was seated at her desk at The Post when she received a very interesting phone call. It was from a private investigator whom she had closely worked with on numerous occasions.

"Ms. Engres, I got a call from a close associate of mine that I thought would interest you," he said. "I thought I should fill you in."

She smiled. She had been ready for something like this. "Yes, go ahead."

"A man by the name of Martin Lamb has been doing some checking into your personal life." The man paused before he continued. "I don't know if you know him, but I would want a heads up if I were you."

She cleared her throat. "Thank you, but it's nothing. Official business; I was expecting it." She hung up the phone and continued to smile. Martin Lamb was President DeSai's, right-hand man. My, my, Cyril didn't waste any time, did he?

While Rasia was tempted to dig and discover what he was trying to learn, she was unsure who his supporters were and who in the world was untouched by his seeming control. It would not do to send up red flags. She did not want him to discover her true motives in any way, so she opted to ride it out for the time being.

There was only one thing that bothered her: his gaze. It was intensely powerful, and she could imagine that all who had fallen under it had become his almost instantly. This was why men, but especially women, were at his beck and call: he controlled them with his mind, and he used his eyes to accomplish this. Nothing in the Book had prepared her for its intensity, but how were her ancestors to know? They were even unsure of his very existence. Until now, the vampire was only a longing and a fantasy in the mind of the witch.

Right then, Rasia decided to read and re-read the Book from front to back. She had cast the spell of protection, but she needed its knowledge to be as strong as she suspected she really needed to be, so when she returned home that evening she began. She also repeated the protection spell on a nightly basis, strengthening herself and the gate which the Powers had surrounded her with.

She would not fail; she began to detail the final pieces of her plan to own him fully and completely.

In the meantime, Cyril DeSai had become nothing short of obsessed. He discovered, with the help of Martin Lamb, that his fiery redhead was one of the most professional and focused individuals in journalism. He also discovered that she had never had a long-term relationship or a boyfriend to speak of. She was determined and driven. These facts had led the President to fantasize about her possibly being a virgin, which he had always longed for, and he directed all of Martin Lamb's investigations be conducted in a way that may answer this question for him. Normally he would have been able to simply smell whether she was untouched or not, but the room had been far too crowded…

The thought preoccupied him so that he demanded more and more personal information.

He wanted to meet her and spend time alone with her. He was confident he could draw her into his inner circle and make her his own, and the only way he could think of to break the ice and attract her was to bait her with what it seemed she desired: success.

He would offer her the opportunity to interview him privately; yes, it was ingenious. At least, he thought so, that is until Martin informed him that she did not allow herself to be alone with men; that was why she toted that lumbering interference she called a photographer along with her. He would be easy enough to deal with, though. Not only did he look at DeSai like he was a god, DeSai suspected he was no more than a boy in a man's body. He would sic one of his beautiful slaves on the kid and have Rasia to himself.

He could not shake her from his mind, and he had never experienced that before. She consumed his every waking thought, and she filled his dreams in a fashion that tormented him. He did not want other women now, it seemed. He simply used them physically and disposed of them.

The vampire was convinced he had found the queen he had been seeking for centuries, but she fought him. He felt it, and he did not understand how she had the power to resist him. He was confused, angry, and consumed.

Cyril DeSai was in love.

∞

Rasia Engres had developed something of a plan that she believed may help keep her safe from his lure.

She had been invited to interview the vampire and American president Cyril DeSai alone, but she had turned down the offer. She had not done this because she was so much afraid of him 'seducing' her; she would only give up what she wanted to in this life, and as of yet, this was a distant thought. She turned him down to control the situation and reel him in a bit, nothing more. He may be a vampire, but he was still a man, and nothing bothered a man more than rejection from a woman.

Their egos were so fragile. Rasia laughed out loud at this thought.

Just as she suspected, she received yet another call from the lackey Martin Lamb inviting her to interview, and this time she accepted, but under one condition only: Oleks would accompany her. She would not be alone with DeSai under any circumstance. At least, not until she was willing and it suited her personal needs.

She needed him to admit to her what he was, and once she had drawn that information out of him, she would move on to Phase Two of her plan. That would be the final phase; she would either control the throne or seat herself on it, and she would not settle for anything less than one of those two outcomes. She would prefer, however, to rid herself, and the world, of DeSai entirely. Only that way would she be in complete and utter control.

But she was willing to settle if she had to. The very fact that he wanted to see her, even under the guise of a personal interview, was all the proof of his feelings she needed. Men, in general, sickened Rasia Engres, but she would settle temporarily.

She would also kill him in the long run if she had to. She would only go to that extreme if it were at all possible, of course. But first he would need to bite her, and she was sure she could whet his appetite enough to convince him to do it. The interview was scheduled for the day after tomorrow; she had until then to cast the protection spell once again and fortify her personal resolve. This was vital for herself and for her ancestors. The future didn't matter; she had no intention of producing any more witches. Why should she?

She planned to live forever, and falling in love was the furthest thing from her mind.

CHAPTER 20

Vitaly and Rasia sat at a table in the cafeteria of The Post, having their lunch together and chatting.

Suddenly, Rasia looked at Vitaly with excitement in her eyes. "I have a surprise for you, Boss Man," she said to him.

"Yes? What is this surprise?" he asked her as he cut into his chicken with a fork.

She placed her own fork on her plate and sat back against her seat. "I have a one-on-one interview with the new American president."

Vitaly nearly choked on his food. "Cyril DeSai?"

Rasia smiled broadly, amused at Vitaly's child-like demeanor. "Is there another?" she asked, then she said, "Yes, DeSai. I have an interview the day after next, and he will be paying for my travel and lodge expenses. I will be taking Oleks with me, of course. I hope I have your approval?"

"Of course!" Vitaly laughed loudly. "Now Rasia, this is the time to use your personal touch. We want the world to see the man, not the legend." The editor was speaking fast, and he was no longer paying any attention to his meal. "If ever you involved emotion that is positive, now is the time. We want to paint a picture of the "People's President," do you understand?"

Rasia just smiled and shook her head. She felt a bit of disgust, and it came out in her response. "Do you take me for a moron, Vitaly?"

Now the editor looked confused. "No, of course not! You are one of my very best. You have drive, talent, and stamina," he told her. "I have full faith in you to produce an award-winning story on this man. Why would you think that?"

Now her voice took on a snide quality, and it was accompanied by a sneer. "I will not only write a story, but I will also bring DeSai to life for the common reader. For you to expect anything less from me is not only insulting, but it is also infuriating," she said. "Here you employ countless journalists who are living on a professional treadmill, like a bunch of the walking dead, but in me, you have always had the very best. I would bite your tongue, Vitaly before something bites you."

She stood up, leaving her dishes as they were. "Oleks and I will leave in a couple of days. You will get your story upon my return, do you understand?"

He just looked at her with a straight face and nodded. She could be so intimidating. The odd thing was that he had no problem being the boss with anyone else at the paper, but when it came to Rasia, he felt like a child who had been caught with his hand in the cookie jar.

She walked away, smug and satisfied. Stupid, stupid Vitaly! He would get far more than he bargained for.

Oleks and Rasia left on a late flight the very next night; they were due to meet with DeSai at the White House just after lunch the very next afternoon. She wanted them both well rested and on their toes; anything less was unacceptable.

Now she stood in the ladies' room at the Reagan Airport in Washington. She was freshening her makeup and straightening her clothing when she felt the fury inside of her grow suddenly; she was angry at DeSai, she realized. How dare this man possess something so priceless and precious and have so little appreciation for its content and depth. He would never die, so he cared not for the gift's meaning.

Then she considered the fact that he had rung her cell phone the night before, and their brief conversation, while frustrating to her, was also compelling. Had he really called her in the night? Indeed he had.

He was a worthless piece of crap. He was intelligent, sexy, and alluring.

She glanced around at the horde of women around her; she needed to get away from their cloying scents and their giggles. She left the restroom in a rush, breathing in the air of the concourse. How she hated crowds.

She and Oleks fetched the bags and caught a cab, ignoring a limo driver with a large card bearing the name 'Engres.' Rasia directed their driver to the hotel, where DeSai had reserved two rooms for them. The place was quite magnificent, Rasia had to admit. Just standing in the lobby and checking in solidified her belief that this new world was precisely what she longed for. No more running around and asking asinine questions of those who treated her like a beggar. Soon they would all be begging her.

They would stay here three nights, so she unpacked, and she had told Oleks to do the same. Then she dressed in a crisp yet attractive professional brown with pink pinstripes suit, and she put her hair up off her neck. While she didn't want to put him off, she didn't want him overwhelmed, and her hair was one of her very best features. It was best to keep him at arms-length this early in the game.

When she was finished dressing, she grabbed her shoulder bag and went down to Oleks' room. After she fetched him and his equipment, the two went to the lobby to wait for the driver that Martin Lamb had told her to expect. There was the same limousine and driver from the airport. "President DeSai welcomes you," he greeted them, and after a few more words, he put them into the car and soon they were off, heading for the American White House to meet with the newest President and get an interview. Rasia found herself deep in thought during the drive.

She had spent her entire life pursuing 'vampires.' She had learned about them and searched for them. She had been full of hope, and she had given up hope, but here she was, heading to meet with one. While she had no proof that DeSai was one, she knew it in her dark soul. All of her dedication and hard work had paid off, and it was very hard to believe the reality of it. She had a glass of Cabernet from the limo's wet bar to help her relax just a bit. It wouldn't do to be a nervous wreck. After all, she had to keep up appearances. Oleks tried to have one as well, but she slapped his hand away and scolded him. She wouldn't allow it; he couldn't hold his liquor as she could.

By half-past twelve, they were pulling into the underground parking garage at the White House where they were met by a pair of Secret Service agents who walked them to the Oval Office. It was official, but very relaxed at the same time. Soon, she would interview Cyril DeSai privately in the next step of her plan to get the only thing she ever wanted.

∞

Cyril DeSai and Rasia Engres met personally for the first time that day. Rasia saw him as a stepping stone; DeSai saw her as a thing of beauty. So enraptured was he that he had to go to the restroom to rid himself of an erection. His penis seemed to have a mind of its own. Never had a woman affected him this way. He made sure he had contained the physical symptoms of his passion for her before he left the bathroom.

They were introduced to him officially when he returned, and the scent of her nearly drove him mad. He immediately gave his attention to the young cameraman she had brought to chaperone her; he wanted her to see that he had the very best of intentions, even though he truly did not, and that was the way to begin.

When he turned to Rasia, he offered her hand a chaste kiss. While she found this a bit entertaining, she was also disturbed. As soon as his lips brushed against her flesh, she had been filled with a certain warmth, and she knew she was blushing. She could not remember a man making her blush, and for a split second Rasia was wondering if there was more to this meeting than what met the eye.

Cyril wanted to give her the impression that he was old-fashioned and respectable. She believed he was old-fashioned; how old fashioned only he truly knew, but respectable? A murdering vampire? Once she had her wits about her, she smiled and nodded curtly. She needed to get down to business and begin the interview so she could refocus, so with pleasantries aside, she suggested they get right down to business. In the initial stages of this dance, it was important to keep him at arm's length if she was going to see this through to the end.

As for DeSai, her cold disposition was highly attractive to him, almost to the point of causing physical pain, and she saw it on his face. For all of his strength and power, this man was so weak! He was like putty in her hands, and she knew right away that carrying out her agenda would be as easy as putting a hot knife through a stick of butter. It was very attractive to her, and this melted even more of her resolve.

So they sat, Rasia distant, Oleks distracted, and DeSai doomed. It was all perfect. Everything was going according to plan.

R.W.K. Clark

CHAPTER 21

Rasia did indeed have an in-depth plan.

It extended far deeper than just sitting by his side and ruling the world, as he obviously intended to do. No, she would not settle. She had outlined her own desires to the Powers very specifically, and she knew that for their own sakes, they would acquiesce to her demands.

She would woo him, much like men did to women. She was doing it already, as she had been, from the moment Vitaly sent her on the assignment to the inaugural press conference. She had been doing it when she initially refused the private interview; and she was doing it now as she sat in this leather chair in the Oval Office in Washington, DC. She was wooing him with her intentional disinterest and cold emotions. She was wooing him by making him earn it.

What did she expect to gain? His obsession. She expected to win his confidence, and she expected to win it to the point that he told her everything about himself and who he really was. She was not willing to simply make assumptions and get herself into a mess with a mortal man who had somehow managed to gain the

Presidency in some manipulative fashion; she wanted his soul and his life eternal, only she was not willing to share it.

She would get from him all she wanted. She would take the eternal life that was his. Then she would stop his rotting heart from beating and take his very place. Nothing less would satisfy her; nothing. But she did not count on falling for him. No, it was not part of her master plan, but it seemed that he was having an effect.

The interview lasted two hours, during which time she asked him the obligatory questions that any journalist would ask if they were in her position. If it came down to turning this in to Vitaly, she would doctor it up, appeal to public emotion, and go from there, but she had no intention of having to turn it in. If she had her way, Oleks would be returning to Kiev and The Post on a solo basis, but not until she got some good photos out of him to save face.

Oleks shot pictures, and she recorded the President's voice as he answered her inquiries. DeSai shared a marvelously spun tale of his life with the two, and Rasia asked all the right questions. It would be a wonderful piece, one that Vitaly could be proud of.

When two hours had passed, Rasia was abrupt in cutting off the meeting. She was so short that it bordered on rudeness, but she didn't know what else to do. As he spoke and she listened to his articulations, she warmed up to him; he even brought her to laughter on more than one occasion. Even though she knew from her research that he was lying to her through his teeth, she understood the reason why, and so it didn't matter. They would be sharing this yarn with the world together.

Rasia had to get out of there. She was enjoying the company of Cyril DeSai way too much.

"Well, thank you President DeSai. We have gotten what we need, and I thank you for your cooperation," she said. "Will your driver be returning us to the hotel?"

Next DeSai played into her hand even better than she anticipated he would. "Your room is covered for three days," he began, and he followed it by inviting her to tour the city, with him as her guide. She refused, and his eyes filled with passion and fire; he was on the verge of dropping to one knee and begging.

She saw her opening and finally accepted his invitation. "You know, I think that would be fine. I'm sure Oleks would enjoy it as well, would you not?"

So it was settled. DeSai laid out his plan to show her some of the sites, and he included Oleks Vanderflute in the plans; he was a smooth one indeed.

Then Cyril fumbled a bit. He brought up a meal at a steakhouse, a tour of his wineries, and even city sites. Rasia remained distant and aloof, calling him 'sir' and holding her smile. She noticed that he continued to try to look her directly in the eye, and when he did, his power flowed. She dodged his stares and maintained personal control.

Suddenly he was inviting them to take their next meal there, an early supper, and Rasia actually agreed. She wasn't sure if it was any power of his making her so agreeable, but she was having a good time. It would also give her a bit more time to work her magic, and it would give the Powers more time to work theirs. The three indulged in a succulent meal prepared by the White House chef, and Oleks remained basically still while Rasia listened to DeSai as he tried to impress her and win her affections.

He asked her questions, both personal and professional, which she answered quite vaguely at first, but soon they were talking pretty openly. He had a way of bringing it out of her. First, he asked her about her family.

"Rasia, is your family in Kiev?" he asked her.

While she was tempted to share all with him, she was also apprehensive. It was not enough to deter him, however. He was picking up on the smallest of details, and from what she could tell and the words he spoke in response, his affections for her were growing. The longer they talked, the more hers grew as well.

"I don't talk about my personal life," Rasia replied.

His response was epic to her; he actually took the upper hand. "I just shared very direct answers to many bold questions with you, but you will not tell me where your parents live?" His tone was stern, and the smile on his face tight and grim. She felt slightly chastised, and it was a bit erotic.

Rasia acquiesced, sharing with Cyril that her parents were not living. The way she replied quieted him, and she went back to her food. It didn't matter; she knew from the way he made her feel that getting closer to him was going to happen; it was just a matter of time.

She finally wrapped up the late luncheon, and they confirmed that the President's car would pick up her and Oleks at the hotel on the morrow, at eleven in the morning precisely. At that time DeSai would indulge them entirely by showing them about, feeding them, and basically showing them the time of their lives.

Rasia gave Oleks the night to himself, and she focused on preparing the story just in case she had to turn it in. She wrote on her laptop with plans to go through Oleks' digital photos later on. She assumed he would head to the bar and have a drink or two, which is all she assumed he could handle. The chubby, lumbering cameraman was cute in his own disgusting way; maybe he would even get laid.

She went to sleep that night feeling a deep-seated satisfaction. Not only were things going smoothly, but they were also going incredibly well. She was feeling an attraction for the American president: he was incredibly intelligent and sexy. He was intuitive, and he could see through her to an extent. She was sure he saw through her emotional game, if not through her ulterior motives. This was good; it would make the execution of her plan so much easier.

Before Rasia finally drifted off to sleep, she made mental plans to wake early and get Oleks over to her room with his camera. They could have a light breakfast, leaving room for whatever fares DeSai would feed them. Lord knew they would have to leave room for his meal if it would be anything like the way he fed them today. Rasia still felt full and a bit bloated from the rich, delicious food.

∞

She woke very early the next morning, refreshed and excited to begin the day. She didn't want to admit it, but she was even a bit eager to visit DeSai. She found herself glad that Oleks would be going along. The last thing she needed this far along in the game was to break her own rules. The man was proving to have a slight effect on her, but she was confident in her own strength. Her personal agenda had driven her too far and carried her too long to ruin it all now because she got horny for the first time in her life.

She dialed Oleks' room but got no answer, so she ordered room service and hopped into the shower. She then sat down to eat the food which had just arrived, and she tried Oleks once again. Still nothing.

She grew angry, which soon turned to fury. They had things to do, dammit! Give the help an inch, and they take a mile! She dressed in jeans and a shirt and left to rouse him. First, she knocked on the wrong one, then went to his room, where she knocked sharply many times, with no response. She hollered through the door, but nothing would wake the cameraman.

Finally, Rasia obtained a duplicate key card from the front desk and unlocked the door herself. She was shocked to find his bags unpacked, and his bed still made. The worthless SOB had gotten drunk and shacked up with some broad, she determined. If he did not return by the time the limo arrived, he was fired, and she had no qualms about that. He was going to make her dine with DeSai on her own, she was sure of it!

She snatched his camera bag from his bed and took it to her room. She would view his shots herself, no problem. He may get fired, but he wouldn't keep the photos, she would see to that! If she had to go to the White House alone, she would. She had faith in the Powers ability to protect her.

She proceeded to edit her article until ten o'clock, and then she dressed for the luncheon. No word from Oleks, and by the time she was ready she had already decided he was unemployed; nothing would change her mind. She checked her appearance in the mirror; she glowed! Even her anger could not steal her beauty, and she was sure her intended victim would agree with her assessment.

When Rasia disembarked from the elevator, the limousine was already waiting, the driver standing at rapt attention by the back passenger side door. After initial greetings, he helped her into the vehicle, and they started off once again. She did try to get in touch with her cameraman several times more, but finally, put it out of her mind. What did it matter? He was her former employee, after all.

Inside, Rasia was greeted by a very affectionate DeSai, who was curious as to where her escort was. She made sure he understood that even though Oleks did not 'feel' like coming, she only maintained their plans as a courtesy. She normally would have never met with a man without him.

They ate together once again, this time discussing a wide variety of very intelligent and interesting topics. Rasia found that she felt more than comfortable with the president that day. Their laughter came easily, and it made the meal and the wonderful wine taste even better.

They also discussed wine, in great detail, during the meal. "Tell me, Rasia, what is your favorite, red or white?" Cyril asked her, a teasing smile on his face. He wanted to see how much she really knew about the various beverages.

"I love both, but red appeals to me more," she stated. "I love its rich dryness, and of course, how could one not be more attracted to such a lovely… color. The color alone is enough to mesmerize me."

Cyril nodded and looked at her over the lip of his own glass. "I would agree."

When the meal wrapped up, he took her on a tour of the city, showing her some sites which she had already seen in her life, but with DeSai they were more interesting, she had to admit. He was a master conversationalist, and he had a wonderful sense of humor. She began to genuinely enjoy his company.

She was tempted several times to ask him personal questions, but the Powers inside held her back. It was not time, she knew. When the time was right, even she would not be able to stop the next step from being taken.

They wrapped up their day together, with plans to

visit the winery the next day. He would give her the ultimate tour, he assured her. If she wanted to bring Oleks, he was welcome, but she knew he would not be coming. She also had a feeling deep inside that tomorrow would be a very special day indeed.

She went back to her room, no Oleks to be found, but she didn't care. She had a feeling that tomorrow's tour would be much, much more than a simple winery tour. At least, if she had her way it would.

R.W.K. Clark

CHAPTER 22

The world, as Rasia Engres knew it, would change drastically. Everything she had ever dreamed of would become hers, and it began with the second tour of the winery.

She spent the day being wooed, and the Powers helped her to play Cyril DeSai into her hands with soft words, wine in a carriage, and long, private talks. She dressed her very best, and he melted into her hands like so much chocolate. He decided to show her his inner sanctum, his private office at the winery that had been his demise.

What Rasia did not expect, what she had not considered in all of her conniving and planning, was that she was going to fall in love with Cyril DeSai that day. No, she had not been in love before, nor did she ever expect to be, but something about the man would win her over completely.

After all of the touring, introductions, and wine tasting, the two were able to begin to talk in earnest. Even though Rasia did not go into honest detail regarding her lineage or who she really was, Cyril was able to warm her up enough to get her to talk during their steak meal together. She was apprehensive at first, but once she began to share with him, she found that he was one of the easiest persons to talk to she had ever encountered.

But it was their carriage ride together with the wonderful wine that really did the trick. Suddenly Rasia began to comprehend what romance was, and the revelation brought her great joy and satisfaction. They sat together on a blanket in the grass, the sun just beginning to set in the sky, sipping wine, laughing, and talking like age-old friends.

"Rasia, I know you are holding back," Cyril said, the breeze blowing gently through a strand of his black hair. "Give me a chance; tell me just a bit about yourself. I long to know the woman inside."

She looked down at the glass in her hands, turning it in circles nervously. Finally, she looked up at him and smiled. "What if you do not like what you hear, Mr. President?"

Now it was Cyril's turn to grin. "I don't think there is a thing you could say to me that would make me draw away from you."

Rasia's green eyes stared into his black ones as she looked for any sign of deception. When she was satisfied that he was genuine with her, she said to him, "I have never liked men, even in the slightest."

Cyril raised his eyebrows in surprise. "You like women?"

Now Rasia laughed aloud. "No, no. That is not what I mean." Her eyes sparkled at his question. "What I mean is that I have never had interest in a relationship with a man, nothing more than a professional one, anyway."

"Why is that, Rasia?" he pressed. "You are strikingly beautiful, intelligent, and successful. There is nothing about you that any man would not admire or desire."

She looked down at her glass once more before draining it of the rich Merlot it contained. Cyril wasted no time in filling it again as she answered him. "It is not that I do not attract them. The issue truly is that I do not care for them as human beings."

"Why not, my Rasia?"

Taking a sip of her fresh wine, she closed her eyes and escaped for a moment in its flavor. Merlot had never been the best, but DeSai's was exquisite. "Throughout my life, they have only approached me with one thing in mind. They have not respected my gifts or my mind, they have only shown interest in my body and appearance."

"They have damaged you," Cyril said quietly.

"No," Rasia replied. "I have damaged them."

The two sat quietly for several minutes before she continued. "From a young age, I have been a very determined person. It also seems I have attracted the attention of all the leaches in existence. They would touch me when I didn't want to be touched, or they would assume I did want to be," she said, pausing for a moment. "It is infuriating to me."

"You have not found a man you trusted with… yourself?" Cyril did not want to appear too eager to obtain this information, but it was the perfect time to ask.

He would receive no answer right then, though. "So, Cyril, what about you. Tell me a secret of yours. Tit for tat, you know."

"Ah, Rasia, tit for tat," Cyril replied with a grin. "Let's see; what is a 'safe' secret I could share that wouldn't endanger world peace or national security?"

Rasia continued to look at him as he pondered. He was indeed a handsome man, and he was articulate and real. She felt safe with him, and this was not a feeling that she was accustomed to. It made her feel warm, cared for, and very secure.

"I have a cave in Honduras that I often visit to have solitude," Cyril finally said.

Now Rasia's eyebrows raised. "A cave?"

DeSai nodded. "Yes. Not a private island or a luxury resort, but a cave."

"Tell me, why a cave?" She watched him closely, trying to see any change in his facial expressions.

Cyril shrugged, and for a moment he resembled a nervous teenaged boy. "I guess because I like the darkness, and the coolness in the air there calms me."

"I would like to visit that place sometime, Cyril," Rasia said in a husky voice.

He nodded at her. Cyril said firmly. "And you shall, Rasia Engres. You shall."

DeSai stood and reached for her hand to help her to her feet. "But for now, I still have things to show you here. Shall we?"

Rasia took his hand eagerly and rose to her feet. She drained the wine from her glass in one gulp, then handed the glass to her host. Cyril took it and then offered her his elbow with a smile. "It wouldn't do to get you so drunk you fall down and soil your dress. Take my arm and steady yourself."

She did so, giggling the whole time. She felt like a young girl with a crush on a rock star. She felt giddy and happy. She felt like, after all her years on the planet, she may have found her very first best friend.

The carriage ride back to Cliffside was just as fulfilling. Cyril knew how to talk to her, but better than that he knew how to listen.

"Tell me about your parents, Rasia. Were they as driven and determined as you?" he asked.

"I didn't know my father," she began. "He died before I was born. My mother died not so long ago, but we were not close. I suppose she was a determined woman in her way, so I likely got it from her."

DeSai continued to watch the path before them as they moved. "I would guess you are much like her, really. Maybe that is why the two of you were not close."

"I have never liked weakness, particularly in females," Rasia told him. "She had areas of weakness that I had no time for."

Once again, the two fell into silence. Rasia laced her arm through his and lay her head on his shoulder, closing her eyes. He smelled so good, and she could feel his strength through his clothing. If this was love, she was all for it.

Cyril looked down at her face, and his heart melted. She was perfect, like a porcelain doll. He would make her his wife, and she would be the queen of his people. Together they would rule the world, prospering and guiding their children into all that eternity had for them.

Yes, it was love for them both.

∞

They arrived at the winery, and immediately, DeSai took her by the hand, and they got on the elevator, but this time he pressed the button to go down. After a bit of verbal fumbling and nervousness, their lips came together, softly at first, as the elevator moved slowly lower and lower. Softness turned into a passion, and passion to desperation. Both of them embraced their lips and tongues exploring each other's mouths.

The elevator came to a stop, and the doors slowly opened. Rasia was immediately taken aback by the décor in the long hallway leading to the black double doors. The walls seemed to be alive with scenes of violence and evil. The sculptures on the pedestals which ran along both walls were unlike anything she had ever seen: demons and gargoyle-type creatures ravaged fair maidens without guilt or shame. Her mouth was open in wonder, and her eyes wide with adoration.

"Cyril, I have never seen things so beautiful in all my life," she whispered.

She turned to him fully. "Cyril, I need to tell you something. Cyril, I am a virgin," Rasia said breathlessly as she pulled away from him.

DeSai touched her face with his hand, caressing her skin as he looked into her eyes. "We have all the time in the world. Do not worry."

Goosebumps broke out over the vampire's body. "You like my taste in art. These are very dark works, Rasia."

"Nothing else would do," she said simply. Now she released his arm and began to walk slowly down the length of the corridor, stopping at each piece to touch and admire it. "The walls. I have never seen anything like it. It is so real; it is a masterpiece in and of itself."

Cyril simply stood by the elevator door at the mouth of the corridor, his arms crossed over his chest and a smile on his face as he watched her. Could this woman be real? Could he have really found someone so like himself? She could not be more perfect!

When she reached the doors at the end of the hall, she turned to him, her eyes lit up with zeal. "This is your office. I cannot wait to see inside, Cyril."

With that, he shoved his hands into his trouser pockets, a shy, boyish smile on his face.

When he opened the office door, Rasia inhaled sharply. It was filled with much of the same type of art, but it was darker and more disturbing than all the rest. She loved every bit of it, from the wonderful pieces to the desk and two chaise lounges before the blazing fire.

Rasia Engres had come home.

She walked around the room, soaking up as much of the beautiful information as she could.

"Sit, Rasia." She nodded at him and sat on one of

the lounges, her gaze continuing over the entire room.

"Rasia, there are things I need to tell you," Cyril began.

She pulled her eyes away from the walls and furnishings, looking at him directly. "Yes, Cyril. I am listening."

With that, he began. Cyril shared with her about his winery in France and his beautiful wife and children who were brutally murdered. For the first time in her life, Rasia shed a tear for another human being, and DeSai cried with her, grieving the loss of his family for the first time in centuries. He told her the truth about everything; his desire to have a true family that would last forever, and the way he had to go about getting it.

They sat in his inner office talking for some time. He came completely clean with Rasia, the love for her showing powerfully in his eyes. She entranced him, and she felt a powerful stir at all of his words. This man had suffered great emotional trauma, and he had carried it with him for years. Yes, he was a vampire, he was a monster, but when Rasia looked at him, all she saw was a lonely man.

She rose and moved over by him, holding his hand as he spoke to her about the pain he had endured for hundreds of years. The loneliness and hollowness he carried with him daily must have been horrid for him, but Rasia Engres thought she understood better than he could imagine. She was not a vampire, but she had been hollow and lonely ever since she could remember. She had simply used it to her advantage, just as he had. They were two very similar creatures indeed.

Next, he shared with her how he had roamed the Earth for centuries, seeking only to build his family, which he was now in the process of doing again. Recently, he had been looking for his one true Queen.

He had found her. When he revealed this to her, which also gave away his true feelings for her, his eyes lit up with a raging fire of love and desire. It surprised her that the vampire her ancestors had sought could feel anything that resembled love, but when she looked into his eyes, she saw it there, and there was no mistaking it.

Then she shared her past with him as well, but not to the extent that he went with her. She told him about her lust for blood and violence, but only regarding men. She shared with him about her longing for power and control, and how she was going about getting it. She even told him that her intentions with him had started out being less than admirable, but she admitted eagerly that her feelings had changed.

She believed she was in love with Cyril DeSai, and she wouldn't have it any other way.

The only thing she did not tell him was that she was a witch. What if that fact obliterated his feelings for her? What if he knew something she did not? Maybe witches and vampires were forbidden to be together? No, she would keep it to herself until they belonged to each other entirely. Then it would be too late.

The two talked for hours. They shared their most intimate truths with each other, and they cried and laughed together like a couple of long lost friends finally reunited. Nothing had ever seemed so perfect for either one of them.

"You are the queen I desire, Rasia," Cyril told her finally, gazing deep into her eyes. "I am yours."

He would give her all she wanted: power, money, eternal life. She only needs to succumb to him, and for the low, low price of emptiness for all eternity. He did not understand that Rasia had been black and hollow her entire life, and she enjoyed it.

"Nothing you are offering me comes as a cost," she said, touching his cheek. "I know what I am inside, and what you will give me will only make it better."

Their lovemaking began with his lightning-speed movements. He was upon her in the blink of an eye, his hand filled with her hair, his mouth on hers. Soon, he was feeling her body from top to bottom, and from the hot tingle between her legs, she knew all at once she was going to like every minute of what was to come. She had shared the fact of her own virginity with him, and this had satisfied him to no end. They both considered the situation to be perfect for each of their own selfish needs.

Once they were naked, they gazed at each other; Rasia had to admit, she had never seen a man so good-looking in all her life. The sight of him all but stole her breath, and she felt the powerful flutter of love, both in her heart and in her body. She was ready for him to take her, and she was eager to begin her new life with him.

After they both filled their eyes with the sight of each other, Rasia dashed at him, wrapping herself around him and kissing him hard, her tongue licking his. She scratched at his back and ran her fingers into his hair, and Cyril could feel her raw, honest desire. He seemed to lose all control over himself with the emotion.

Finally, he picked her up off the ground and carried her to the lounge that sat before the fire. He laid her down upon it; he needed to prepare her for his taking. He buried his head between her legs and began to lick and kiss her like she had never known. Yes, she had been naturally nervous, and still was to an extent, but she responded to his mouth and the love he was giving her with intensity. Her hips bucked against his face, her hands tangling in his hair. She clawed at him in pleasure as he brought her to climax again and again.

Then, with a move as fast as lightning, he was on top of her. She could feel his hardness brushing against her thighs, and even though she did not know what to expect, she was ready. Her hips arched against him, and she moved until she felt the head of his manhood at her core. They both thrusted together at precisely the same moment, and after a flash of pain, he was inside of her. She gasped, but the pain faded as quickly as it had arrived.

Oh, she had never felt anything like it. It was all-encompassing: physical, mental, and emotional. It was as though she was one with this man, and their movements were proof. She was aware of every breath he took, the feel of his skin, and the sounds he made as he moved on and in her. If she had doubted whether or not she was in love with Cyril DeSai, she did not doubt any longer; she was his and his completely.

Before she understood what was happening, the tingle between her legs began to grow into the heat of a fire, and suddenly, she was overtaken by the savage orgasm that his strokes brought. She clung to him, thrusting against him, her eyes wide open with shock and surprise. She had no idea it felt like this, and she wanted more right away.

It didn't take long. He continued to move inside of her, and even reached down and stroked her with his fingers as he did. She cried out; Rasia was going to come yet again. As it overwhelmed her, Cyril took action, and with perfect timing he bit her, giving her that special bite, the one that would make her his queen for all eternity. It was sharp like glass and painful, and she was acutely aware of the rushing of her own blood as it began to pound painfully through her brain.

Suddenly she was changing, there was no mistaking it. She felt intense strength and an even more powerful lust. She could feel her own flesh somehow alter, going from temporal to eternal, cell by cell. It was painful, but it brought her pleasure, and she threw back her head, her mouth wide as she reveled in the feeling of her mortal body dying.

Then she felt something else, as well. All of her anger, her personal insanity, and her black soul grew within her at an alarming rate. All at once she loved him, but she hated him with a passion for the fact she would have to submit to this man for all eternity. The emotional mix was one she had no personal control over. As she tried to sort through it all, Cyril's body went stiff; he was coming inside of her, and she felt the rage that was building boil over.

He lay on top of her, gasping for breath and shuddering with pleasure. She stroked his hair and his skin, a hateful smile on her face as she did so. Yes, she loved him. Oh, how she suddenly hated him! How to feel? She did not need to wonder, for her feelings would soon reveal it to her.

Cyril sat up and looked into her eyes. "Are you okay, my Rasia?"

"Yes, Cyril," she told him with a peace that was not customary. "I couldn't be more perfect." She was even smiling.

Rasia knew it was time, as the Powers took control of her, though she knew not for what. She reached up and wove her fingers into his black hair, and kissed him hard as she got a firm grip on his head. Then, before she even knew what she was doing, and before he knew what was happening, in one fluid movement, she ripped his head away from the rest of his body. It fell to the floor, blood flowing out of his gaping neck.

But deep inside she knew something very bad had just happened. She felt a small twinge of something like remorse, the fury began to subside, and the regret began to grow. Suddenly it took over, and she collapsed on the empty chaise lounge and began to sob.

What had she done?

It was no longer her intent for this to happen! Cyril

DeSai's lifeless body was on the floor next to the lounge, blood pouring onto the carpeting, and she had no idea how it had happened. She cried with no control, and during that time the Powers began to speak to her soul. The darkness of her own spirit had completely overpowered any love she had inside of her for the man, and now all of her selfish desires had their way. Less than an hour ago, she had been thinking about a future with this man, and now he was dead on the floor before her, by her own hand.

They were one, and even though he was dead, it would be her own hell to endure. She cried at the top of her lungs, tears pouring down her cheeks, as she gathered his blood and grieved the loss of the only person she had ever loved and trusted, no matter how briefly.

What had she done?

CHAPTER 23

Thirty years a virgin

Rasia DeSai sat at her desk in her bedroom reading her Book yet again, going over the history of the women who came before her. They were the witches, just as she was. They had a dream and a vision for the future of their kind, and she had fulfilled it through focus and hard work.

For a woman who had spent thirty years a virgin, she was now overwhelmed with lust, and she spent her days ruling the world, and her nights indulging herself and feeding her passion.

Rasia did not comprehend the lust inside of her. Initially, she had struggled to understand. Nothing in the Book had spoken of it. Nothing in her own studies had ever even suggested that it would happen, or even that it was part of vampirism. She tried on several occasions to take it to the Powers for answers, but they remained uncharacteristically quiet on the issue.

Of course, they would! They were enjoying the sacrifices she brought them. They would do nothing to jeopardize their own satisfaction.

After murdering and sacrificing hundreds of men,

and abusing thousands of women, she came to understand the truth: her purpose had not been just the meeting of the goal. Her purpose had not been to bring countless sacrifices to the Powers. No, her purpose was encapsulated in her secret, but it was not so much a secret anymore.

She closed the Book and sat back. She put her hand on her swollen belly and stroked it, feeling an emotion that was the closest thing to love she was capable of without the presence of her husband. She would bear the child of Cyril DeSai, and this child would be the true ruler of the world for all ages to come.

Rasia locked the Book back in the confines of the safe and stood up from the desk awkwardly. She continued to contemplate all that was before her.

My own personal greed and selfishness in reveling in the craft for my own gain were what the Powers used as a means to an end. A very specific end.

∞

That night while she slept, she had a dream.

Rasia DeSai, the Queen, was at an airport, and she was waiting on the arrival of a flight. Who was getting off the plane she did not know, but she waited eagerly at the gate. Eventually, the plane she was waiting for landed, and the people began to file off, their faces blank stares, and they had no mouths.

Suddenly a young boy with black hair and black eyes got off, and he was without accompaniment. Rasia knew: this was her child. The child she made with the Master, Cyril DeSai. The boy looked as she would have imagined her husband looked like a child; there was no mistaking him for anyone else.

She also knew right away that the boy would rule over her. His name was to be Lucien. She broke into tears right in the terminal, dropping to her knees. A voice, angry, spoke to her:

"Who do you think you are, weak woman? Stand, for you disgust me!" She looked up with fright in her eyes. The speaker was the boy Lucien. She knew his name as well as she knew his father's and her own.

She stood, but her head continued to hang low. She felt shame mingled with disappointment and anger, and suddenly things became very clear to Rasia, terrifyingly clear.

The anger inside was what had driven her all this time. Because of that anger, she had met the goals that had been set out for her to meet by the Powers.

Rasia woke violently, sitting up and gasping for breath. She understood now why she had killed the only man who ever loved her. The lust that had grown in her to monstrous proportions after she had murdered Cyril? It was because this beast growing inside of her was lust. He demanded to be satisfied, and there was no satisfying him.

The boy Lucien was pure, unadulterated evil.

She continued to sit straight up in her bed, fully awake, sweat pouring from her head. Her long, red hair was soaked and matted, and the child in her belly was struggling inside of her. She panted in the darkness and fought to get her wits about her. When she was back to reality completely, she got up and went into her bathroom in the darkness. She drank water in great gulps and took a towel to her face. Then she went into her room and turned on the light. She set candles alight and placed them around the Circle that was embedded in the tiles of the floor beneath her bed. Finally, she fell to her knees and began to beg the Powers for mercy.

For the first three hours of her pleading, they remained quiet. Then, angry, they lashed out from the center of the Circle. They filled her mind with visions that represented their response. They were disgusted.

Did she really believe she was here to satisfy herself? Nothing about her existence was for her. Neither was Cyril's, nor her ancestors' before her. No one on Earth was there for their own fulfillment or pleasure. No, and the success she had experienced was proof of that.

Rasia came out of her trance-like state, the child inside of her kicking violently. A voice came to her head and demanded she be still; the child would not be born for six more weeks. It was her duty now to prepare herself for the task that was to come, and that meant nothing to her own happiness. She needed to rise and calm herself, or the child would be born now, and the process would tear her limb from limb.

Rasia quieted herself except for a few small sobs. She got up off the floor and made her way back to her bed, where she lay back down and stared at the ceiling. Nothing in the Book had ever prepared her for this. It was all a glorious lie.

Who was this child she was destined to bear? The

child of Cyril DeSai, the vampire, and Rasia Engres, the witch? That may be biologically so, but Rasia DeSai, Madam President and Queen, had great doubts. She had no idea, but she firmly knew and believed at that very moment that the child inside of her did not belong to her at all.

She tossed and turned, sweaty and confused, for another hour before she finally fell into a fitful sleep that was filled with distress and unsettling dreams. She saw visions of painful sex and blood, she saw pictures of rotting death and the corpses that resulted. She dreamed of her husband, loving her from the abyss, and though she reached out for him as she saw him, she would never be permitted to touch him. It was torture.

For the first time in her entire life, Rasia felt true fear. How she desired her dead Cyril now… but he was never, ever to live again.

Cyril DeSai, Master of the Vampires, was my husband. I put him to his death.

I am Rasia DeSai, the Queen of Cyril, and ruler of the world.

I am pregnant with his son.

This child will be part vampire part witch, and his name will be Lucien DeSai.

He will come to take the throne.
He is coming soon…

R.W.K. Clark

EPILOGUE

Now Rasia DeSai resided in the White House, She was the Queen of the world, all of its inhabitants her slaves, and her child would rule by her side.

She would have a boy. He would be Lucien, and he would be the only being Rasia would ever love. She accepted this fully once the Powers had words with her. After all, to battle the Powers was pointless; they ruled all things on Earth utterly and completely.

She determined in her heart to make a life for her son that was worthy of him.

Rasia sat down at her desk, and she removed the Book. She began at the beginning and, stroking her belly with love, she read it for the hundredth time, slowly and with purpose. The lust inside of her still burned, even as she read, but the Powers had forbidden her to seek satisfaction. No human male seed was to ever be inside of her until her child was born.

She read with intent. Rasia had the Book memorized, but she read it with love each time she read it. After all, it was her history, and the partial history of Lucien, the child she would bear.

When she completed the very last entry, which was

one of her own spells. The one she had written to request protection from Cyril before going to the press conference. She picked up her pen and began to write on the next blank page, the only thoughts in her mind consumed by a grieving love for the husband she had murdered, and the need to record his contribution to what was to be.

Cyril, her perfect husband, how she now grieved him! To be given the bite that he had given her was a rare gift, a one-time thing for the 'master.' Yes, he had bestowed that gift on her and made her his wife; the rest of the world, indeed, the 'family,' knew it.

ENTREATY

This book was made possible by reviews from readers like you. Reviews fuel my creativity. If you enjoyed this novel, I implore you to please write a review and share your experience on the retailer's website. The livelihood for authors is entirely dependent on reviews, and I must say, it is the largest obstacle as a struggling author that I have encountered. Please tell a friend, tell a loved one about this read. With your help, I will be one step closer to overcoming this obstacle. In return, I thank you from the bottom of my heart, and sincerely appreciate your time and effort.

Humbled, with gratitude,

R.W.K. Clark

ABOUT THE AUTHOR

I am a father of two beautiful children, Jon and Kim. They are my motivating forces; they are the lighthouse in this vast ocean. In my life, they are the air that I breathe; they are the oasis in this desert of uncertainty. They are my greatest joy in life and my number one priority. I have a long list of hobbies, and I attribute that to my lust for life! I like to surround myself with positive people, who share the same interests. Family values, the arts, outdoors, nature, and travel are tops on my list. I embrace attending cultural and artistic events because I believe dramatic self-expression is the window to the soul. I wear my heart on my sleeve, and I still believe in chivalry, and I always treat people the way I want to be treated.

www.rwkclark.com